When Bad Bitches Link Up 2

Iisha Monet

© **2018**

Published by *Miss Candice Presents*

Hey Babies! I just would like to say thank you all for supporting me thus far. You all make a girl from Springfield, Mass feel special. This series meant alot to me and because you all seem to love it so guess what?! Satin and Dream will be getting a spinoff in the near future. See how these ladies takeover Miami. Thank you all for reading!

Also I just want you all to know it's okay to be a woman in man's world. Don't settle for the cliches. Be your true authentic self. The world is your playground, embrace it.

Iisha Monet

Previously in When Bad Bitches Link up

Joi

Surgery was a success and I was ready to recover at home. I hated the hospital with a passion. It just seemed so gloomy and to me, nothing good ever came from being here. Watching Satin and Dream get my things together I smiled at my girls. They really had my back and I appreciated them more than they could possibly imagine.

I did see Jacob. He came by and visited me but I honestly would've preferred for him not to. I was no longer in love with him and I realized that when I saw the lipstick smudge on his shirt. His cheating no longer phased me I honestly just wished he'd do us both a favor and go away. He no longer fed my soul. I no longer craved him. The only thing he did was disgust me.

"You ready sunshine?" Dream asked as she parked the wheelchair in front of me.

"Yeah, I'm ready to get out of here. I hate this damn place."

"Well, in that case, let's get you out of here."

"Izzy's outside already. I got your discharge papers by the way," Satin spoke as she doubled check the room making sure she grabbed all of my belongings.

"Let's blow this popsicle stand!" I joked.

"Joi.. I swear you suck at tellin' jokes. That was so white and corny of you," Dream giggled.

Getting into the wheelchair, I was wheeled out by Dream as Satin walked to the right of us. Words couldn't describe how happy I was to be going home. There's nothing like being in the comfort of your own home granted Jacob was going to be there but I was just going to act like he didn't even exsist.

Since my accident, I said I was going to do any and everything to protect my peace. I should never be so distracted to the point where I put myself in harms way like I did that day. So anyone who wasn't good for me had to go immediately and I meant that. I don't care who they were they had to go. Stressing and worrying about shit was a thing in the past and I just wanted to let it all go. I was going to see a lawyer as soon as I got better just so I can start the divorce process. It was time.

"Heyyy my love!" Isabella greeted as she smiled at me.

"Hey my Izzy bear," I replied back as her and Dream helped me get into the passenger seat then closing the door.

"I haven't told y'all but thank you. I appreciate y'all. I swear I do."

"Girl boo, you don't have to thank us. That's what friends are for. We got ya back. Know that," Dream said.

"Y'all. I ain't even tell y'all what happened with me," Satin started to say.

"What happened to you?" I asked.

"Listen and I'll tell you. So the other morning I was getting dressed to go handle my business and Hassan calls me on Facetime. We sitting there shooting the shit laughing and whatnot and I hear a bitch in the background."

"Wait what?"

"I heard a girl in the background and it wasn't the hoe that we met in Miami either. Anyways you know me, I start asking questions and boom the nigga tells me it's his girlfriend."

"Are you really surprised though Satin? The first time we saw him he was with a bitch," Isabella said as she drove to my house.

"I'm not surprised but I tried hinting at him possibly having a girlfriend a few times and he kept saying he wanted a girl like me so I assumed the bastard was single."

"I mean you shouldn't really be mad if you weren't interested in him like that. Unless yo ass fucked around and fell for him," Dream said and Satin remained quiet. "Bitch you fell for his foreign ass didn't you?"

"I.. I.. His dick is good. I couldn't help it," Satin whined and we all began laughing.

"This girl done went and got dick whipped and caught feelings. At least somebody managed to come along and tear down those walls your mean ass had built," Isabella giggled.

"I need some damn dick. Ima be a damn virgin by time I get laid. Pussy gonna be rejecting the dick." I said as I continued to laugh.

"Well, I happen to be very well taken care of," Dream bragged.

"I bet. That big ass piece of man be manhandling you, huh Dream?"

"Do he! My poor lil coota cat be sore as hell. Got me wondering why did I wait so long to let his fine ass tap this ass. I haven't been seeing much of him lately. He hasn't really been in town. I think he got a bitch somewhere."

"And you got a bitch here. So y'all even," Satin said.

"Why you tellin' my business Satin? I'm not dating that girl," she said bashfully.

"That girl got a name and she was after you with her handsome ass. Shit, I can't blame you if you did dip in the lady pond."

"Dream, since when you start dating bitches?" Isabella asked her as she looked in the rear view mirror at Dream and I started laughing.

"I'm not dating her!"

"You doing something if she's in the picture. I told you your ass was gay!" I joked.

"I'm not gay though. I didn't approach her she approached me. Besides she's a stud so does it really count?"

"She got a pussy, right? Then it fucking counts."

"I don't like you bitches. I'm not gay."

"You're right. You're not. You like dick too much. Your ass is curious though. Did you kiss her?" Satin asked her as I noticed that we had finally made it to my house.

"Once. Leave me alone Satin. I don't know why I even said anything.," Dream pouted getting out of the car.

"I'm not judging boo. Do ya thing. Just let me know if women eat pussy better than a man. I might want to try that shit out since I'm having bad luck with men."

"Something is really wrong with y'all," I said as Dream handed me my crutches so I could walk to the door. "Satin over here bussin her pussy open for strangers, you kissing dykes and Isabella gettin thick on our asses."

"I am gettin' thick though. It's that happy weight. I need to chill before I can't fit my clothes."

"You're fine Izzy. I like you kinda thick. You don't look like a little girl anymore." Dream said as we entered my house and it was a mess. I wasn't even gone for that long and the nigga had my shit looking like a pig sty. Nasty bastard.

As the girls went into the kitchen I hopped my ass around my house checking to see if Jacob's bum ass was there and so far he was nowhere to be found which was a good thing. Finally making my way to my bedroom door I noticed it was cracked open but I know I left it closed.

"Joi, you need to sit down," Satin said coming up behind me but I ignored what she was saying.

Something in me was telling me not to open the door but I had to. It would kill me if I didn't. Pushing the door open what I saw was something I wasn't prepared to see. I damn near threw up in my mouth. This dirty ass nigga had violated and had to fucking go!

"REALLY JACOB? A FUCKIN MAN?!" I yelled and Satin came behind me and looked like a deer caught in headlights.

"KORI?" she yelled and before I knew it I had lost it.

Dream

"KORI?!" I heard Satin yell and Isabella and I hurried and made it to where the commotion was coming from. If Kori hoe ass was up to no good I was beating some ass. She been on some funny shit lately and if what I think is going down is going down then I know why. Bitch was fuckin' her homegirl's husband. Shit shady as fuck.

Finally making it to where everyone was at my heart instantly broke for Joi. I couldn't even imagine how she was feeling at the moment. Her husband was fucking with her friend who just so happens to be a man. I mean nobody knew Kori was born a man but still. There's certain things about her that makes her manly to me.

"Jacob, you like boy pussy now? Hmm?" Joi asked as she chuckled to herself looking crazy.

"Fuck is you talkin' bout?" he asked as he threw on a t-shirt.

"Boy Pussy. Dookie shute. Asshole. You like that type of shit huh? I mean you have to, right? You've been fuckin' a whole man this entire time."

"Fuck is she talkin' bout Kori?"

"I.. I.. Uh.. Baby.." Kori stammered over her words and I rolled my eyes.

"The. Fuck. Is. She. Talkin'. Bout. Bitch?" Jacob asked Kori as he grabbed her by the neck.

"Get to fuckin' talkin'!"

"I.. I.. You know I love you, right? And you love me too, right?"

"Come on Kori. Tell the man that you love you were born a man," Joi taunted.

"BITCH!" Jacob yelled as he started choking Kori out and Satin immediately jumped in playing captain save a hoe as usual.

"Jacob chilllll!" Satin yelled as she struggled to pull him off of Kori and you could tell she was struggling.

After about a minute or two Satin had finally succeeded with pulling Jacob off of Kori but not before he backhanded the fuck out of her. I ain't even gonna lie, that shit looked like it hurt. I honestly didn't feel bad though. Kori is always getting herself into some shit then regretting it later.

"STAY THE FUCK AWAY FROM ME YOU FUCKIN' FAGGOT!" Jacob yelled at Kori before storming out as Kori stood there crying.

"Kori get out," Joi told her calmly as she tried to hold herself up with the crutches. She looked uncomfortable as hell.

"I'm sorry. I'm so sorry."

"Get out of my house."

"Joi, I'm so sorry. I just, I love him. You knew this. He was mine first," Kori cried and I wanted to slap her ass again.

"You love him? He was yours first? Bitch are you fucking hearing yourself right now? Kori, we're all friends. You're fucking pathetic and miserable as fuck. Yeah, we knew you had a thing for fuckin' other people's men but damn bitch we never thought you'd do the shit to one of us," I told her with disgust dripping from my voice.

"You foul as fuck Kor and you know it. Like I don't get it. How could you?" Satin asked in disbelief.

"What you mean how could she? She's fuckin trashy as fuck, that's how. Ain't no limits when it comes to her. Ain't that right Kori?"

"Dream shut up! Instead of worrying about my business you need to worry about your own. You act like your shit don't stink yet you're entertaining a whole bitch. Live your fucking truth. Ain't that what you tell everybody?"

"Bitch!" I yelled and ran up on Kori and slapped her.

"You's a shady bitch. Don't worry about what I got going on. My business is exactly that. My muthafucking business, not yours!"

"KORI. GET OUT NOW! " Joi yelled interrupting us. Kori grabbed her things quickly and left.

Joi was good cause crutches or not I would've dug into Kori's nasty ass. Bitch was wrong on all fuckin' levels. What happened to boundaries? The sister code? Shit was spooky.

"Joi.. are you okay?" Satin asked her.

"Leave! All of you. Just, just leave."

"We're not going nowhere," I told her as I folded my arms across my chest.

"We're your friends, ain't no way we just gonna let you go through this shit by yourself. Nah!"

"I want to be alone. Please don't fight me on this Dream. Just leave," she said and hopped away heading to the guest room and shutting the door.

I understand her being upset but we're friends. We got each other backs. Whether we disagree with each other or not we still have each other's back no matter what. She clearly needs us yet she's going to act like she doesn't. It could be the embarrassment of it all but we're not here to judge her.

"Come on y'all let's clean up this mess before we go. At least her house will be cleaned," Isabella suggested and Satin sucked her teeth.

"Shouldn't do shit for her ass, she kicked us out," Satin pouted and I couldn't help but laugh.

"Now is not the time for you to be petty Satin," I told her.

"Right. Just help us clean so we can go. It'll be quick," Isabella agreed with me as we all took on a room to tackle. I swear I felt like I just watched an episode of Jerry Springer.

****

"Mmmm this feels so good. Thank you," I moaned with my eyes closed as Sosa gave me a foot massage. We were sitting on her couch and my pedicured feet were resting comfortably in her lap. After Isabella dropped Satin and I off I immediately drove to see her. I needed some TLC and since Mega was still out of town Sosa was the next best thing.

"You know you don't have to thank me ma. It's my pleasure. So wassup? You seem bothered. Anything I could help you with?" she responded back to me.

"No. Not really. It's nothing, just girl drama. You know how that goes."

"Yeah I do, that's why I hang with a bunch of niggas."

"So you tellin' me you don't have any female friends?"

"Nah, I mean I have you but I wouldn't call you a friend. You're someone I'm interested in," she mentioned.

I gave her a nervous giggle as her hand traveled up my leg tracing my inner thigh causing me to shiver. *This is what happens when your hot pussy ass decides to come over here with no panties in a dress.* I thought as I looked at her with lust filled eyes.

I was feeling butterflies. Nervousness yet I didn't stop her. I didn't want to and the more she touched me the more open I got. Parting my legs a little bit, I bit down on my bottom lip as I felt her hand graze over my cookie. My body was on fire. I was horny and whatever Sosa wanted to do to me I was going to let her. I was going to let her have her way with me.

Stopping at my opening she looked at me with a smirk on her face in a cocky manner and I swear I could've came on myself. Sosa was fine. She looked better than most niggas and every time I looked at her I couldn't deny the attraction. *If only she was a man.* I thought to myself as I thought about how perfect we would be together. How good we would look together.

She was the opposite of Mega. Mega was a man's man. He was gentle with me but he was also a thug ass nigga when needed to be. He was what every woman wanted and I had that, yet here I am with a woman who was just as amazing as him. She wasn't all sappy and stuff but she was sweet. Caring. Genuine and as her fingers penetrated my opening she was gentle.

"Ohhhhh," I cooed softly as I watched her watch me. She wasn't going to fast or slow. It was just the right amount of momentum.

She rotated her fingers in a circular motion as they moved in and out of me and out of habit I lifted up my shirt, bringing my hands to my titties and began caressing my nipples. With the sensation I was feeling from both I knew it wouldn't be long before I was cumming all over her hands but then she stopped and I looked at her like she was crazy.

"W-w-what did you do that for?" I asked her confused.

"Can I taste you Dream?" she asked me with her fingers resting inside of me and I nodded my head yes. Removing her fingers she brought them to her lips and sucked my juices off of them.

"Mmmm taste exactly how I imagined you would," she went on to say and before I had a chance to say anything she had dropped to her knees.

"Come here," she demanded and I sat up and positioned myself so that her and my pussy were face to face.

Pulling my bottom to the edge of the cushion of the couch she spread my legs wide as she dipped her head in between my thighs, tasting me. She was licking me slowly all while applying pressure on my clit with her tongue and it was driving me crazy.

"Ssssss," I hissed grabbing ahold of her head and tugging on one of her braids. She was giving me what I needed and I didn't want her to stop.

"Yesssssss," I cried lowly.

"Shit, feel good don't it baby?" she asked me in between licks and I just pushed her head deeper into my cookie answering her question.

I've had my pussy eaten plenty of times but never like this. This was different. She wasn't eating me like she was in a rush. She was taking her time. She was enjoying me and it showed. She was giving me passion with her mouth and I don't think it could've gotten any better than that.

It was feeling so good that my toes were tingling. My legs were going numb. I had never experienced anything like this. A cramp had started to form in the bottom of my stomach as she continued to slurp all on me. I was on my way to experiencing the biggest orgasm I've ever experienced before and I welcomed it.

"Fuckkkkkkkkkkkk," I yelled as my head fell back.

"Oh fuckkkk! Fuckkkkkkk!"

"Mmhmm, let that shit go ma. Let it out," she said into my pussy and as if she had some control over my body, it listened and I began to cum.

"Shhhhhiiitttttttttttttttttttttttttttttttttttt Sosaaaaaaaaaa," I panted.

After a few seconds, she dropped my limp legs and brought her lips to mine and kissed me deeply before taking a seat next to me. Awkward silence filled the air as we both were lost in our own thoughts.

"You aight?" she asked me laughing.

"Y-yeah, I'm okay."

"Ahhh don't start acting shy."

"I'm not. I can't believe that just happened."

"Why not? You ain't enjoy it?"

"I did. I just, I just wasn't-," I started to say as my phone began ringing. Removing it out of my jean jacket pocket Mega's name flashed across my screen and I ignored him.

"What was I saying again?" I asked just as my phone rang again and it was him.

"I gotta take this, give me a second," I told Sosa as I stood up and excused myself walking outside.

He always calling at the wrong time. I thought to myself before answering his call.

"You good?" Mega asked immediately as I answered his phone call.

"Yeah, why?"

"Why you ain't answer the first time?"

"I was doing something. What's up?"

"Like what?"

"Something. What you want Mega? You finally callin' to tell me that you're coming back?" I asked him as I got into the car and drove off. I couldn't chance Sosa coming out and saying anything so I had to leave.

"Wassup with you yo? You good? You got an attitude or some shit?"

"I'm fine, I'm just not with this shit. Nigga, you been gone for how long? Doing random pop-ups like it's gonna make me feel better. I'm over it. Let's quit while we're ahead."

"Fuck is you talkin' bout? I told you what I got going on. You understood from the beginning what you was getting yourself into. Don't go switchin' shit up cause you fucked around and caught feelings. I was callin' to see if you wanted to go away for a weekend but your fuckin' attitude sucks."

"Fuck you! Cause I caught feelings? Really Mega? That's not even the problem. The problem is that I think your big ass is lying. Nigga New York ain't that muthafuckin' far. You're choosing to stay away. You did all this extra shit for what? To get my pussy? Nigga you could've just said you wanted to fuck. Not all this extra shit. Shit mad corny."

"Dream, gettin' pussy ain't shit to me. I can walk outside right now and a bitch will offer to suck my dick just because baby girl. I stepped to you because I think you're dope and I was feeling ya lil fiesty ass. Don't get me wrong, ya lil funky pussy good and all but that pussy ain't movin' me. I fuck with you because I fuck with you. Ima let you cool off. When you ready to talk hit my line, aight?" he said to me but I didn't respond.

"Aight?" he asked again with more authority in his voice.

"Yup!" I said with an attitude.

"You funny yo," he said with a chuckle just before he hung up.

I ain't find shit funny nor was I tryna be. Mega thinks because he got a lil money and he cute or whatever that a bitch gonna be on his shit. Nah not me, I'm the wrong one. Niggas come around every day and I ain't gonna lose sleep because he on some next shit. He can miss me all the way with it.

Mega

I don't know what Dream's issue was but I wasn't the nigga that was gonna entertain the shit. She can have a fucked up attitude all she wants but when business ain't right neither am I. Like I stated before I'm not some punk-ass nickel and dime hustla. I'm out here moving weight and some shady shit was going down in my camp and I needed to get to the bottom of it before I was able to rest comfortably.

I was feeling lil baby somethin serious but she couldn't understand that. Well maybe she could and just didn't want to but either way, I was diggin' the fuck outta her and I had to straighten this shit out so I could focus on her. I know how women like Dream operate. She knows she's attractive and I'm sure muthafuckas shoot they shot every chance they get and her ass entertains it. She's young. She likes attention and since I've been failing to give her that I know she been gettin' it from one of those cornball ass niggas out her way. It's cool though cause as soon as I wrap this shit up, I was dreading all that shit.

Dream can pop all the shit she wants to right now but she knew what it was. I'm official as fuck and fuckin' with a nigga like me isn't an opportunity that gets presented every day. Where she gonna go? To some corny broke ass nigga with a dream to become a rapper? Them niggas can't handle a shorty like her. I put money on that. That's why she all in her feelings now. She knows this. She knows who daddy is and if she doesn't Ima have to remind her ass real soon.

I ain't gon' front though I was probably wrong for saying that caught feelings line but she had pissed me off nagging. I called to talk to her. I called to hear my voice of reason before I went into this meeting on some nut shit and the conversation didn't go as planned as you see.

Putting my phone in my pocket I made my way inside of the warehouse I conduct my business meetings. Here it was almost midnight and I had these muthafuckas out of their beds waiting on me. Some of these niggas probably was just knee deep in some pussy but you think I gave a fuck? Nah. They could suck my dick from the back. Shit was still coming up short and I wanted fucking answers.

"Why are we here?" this lil nigga Ant asked.

"I got other shit I could be doing."

"That's ya word huh A?" I asked as I scratched my beard with a smirk on my face.

"He said he got other shit he could be doing. You hear this shit Mark?" I asked my right hand.

"I hear his pussy ass talkin'. I just want to know what other shit he could be doing. If it ain't about makin' some muthafuckin' money he ain't got shit to do," Mark said as he stood to the right off me.

"Aye Ant, you want to leave?" I asked him but he remained quiet. See I have a pet peeve with shit like that. If I ask you a question I'm expecting an answer. I hate being ignored.

"Ant, I don't like asking a question more than once but I like you so Ima be generous. You want to leave?"

"Yeah nigga, we all want to leave. You got us here in the middle of the night but ain't tellin' us shit," he mouthed off and it made me smile.

Crazy, right? Lil nigga had a lot of balls to talk to me the way he was talkin', right?

"Aight my nigga, you can go," I told him and he began looking around.

"Fuck is you lookin' around for? You said you wanted to go so Ima let you go."

"You serious boss?"

"Yeah, go head. Anybody else want to go with him?"

"Don't you all speak at once," Mark said as he laughed.

I knew nobody wasn't gonna say shit and I also had a naggin' feelin' that this mouthy ass bitch nigga was the one causing me problems. I switched up all my spots but kept the same niggas in charge yet every spot he secured kept coming up short. My eye began twitchin' as I thought about the 300,000 I lost. That's 300,000 dollars I can't get back. I wouldn't even be mad if muthafuckas had a legit reason for stealin' from me. Aight, I'm lyin'. Ima be pissed regardless.

"You leaving or you bout to go?" I asked Ant and instead of responding he looked around once more before making his move to leave but was cut off immediately when I took my gun from my waist and shot him in between his eyes silencing him forever.

"Nigga, you just gon kill the nigga before we get our answers? A corpse can't talk," Mark asked throwing his hands up.

"Nigga was talkin' too much. I never liked his hoe ass anyways. Besides, I think I got my answers," I told him before turning my attention to the thirteen other niggas standing in front of me.

"If my money continues to come up short you'll end up just like ya mans. Clean this shit up. I'm out," I told them as I walked out and got in my Cayenne Porche.

Sorry ass niggas I thought to myself as I pulled off.

Satin

"Kori?" I yelled as I finally made it home. Isabella and Dream had dropped me off earlier but I wasn't in the mood to be home. I didn't want to be alone so I took an Uber to this bar called Theodore's and had some drinks by myself. I was probably looking lonely as fuck but I didn't care. I just wanted to be around people.

Still calling her name I made my way further into our house and saw that nobody was there, or so I thought until I made it to my bedroom and turning on my light where I was met with Hassan's handsome stupid face. I thought I told him to leave me alone. I also thought me blocking his dumb ass from contacting me would give him the damn hint that I didn't want to be bothered.

"Hassan you need to leave."

"We need to talk," he said sounding pitiful as hell.

"We don't need to talk about anything. You need to go before I call the police."

"Call the police and say what?"

"That you're trespassing. Now again, you need to go!"

"It's not trespassing if someone let me in. Your cousin I think it was. She let me in as she was leaving. She looked upset. Is everything okay?"

"Why are you worried about her for? You interested or something? I can set that up. She's a hoe. You're a hoe. Y'all can have the perfect life," I told him as I giggled.

"Are you drunk?" he asked me and I rolled my eyes.

"Satin? You're drunk?" he asked again as he stood up and walked in my direction and I quickly moved tripping over my feet and fell onto the floor.

Extending his arm out to help me I squatted him away. I didn't want him touching me. I didn't want him near me honestly. Hassan was a liar and I don't do liars. I knew he was too good to be true. Between him and Kori, I wasn't sure who was the reason behind my drunkenness. I did, however, know that I couldn't stand either one of their asses.

"I don't need your help. What I need is for you to leave me alone," I snapped.

"I'm not leaving until we talk," he insisted and I released a frustrated sigh. He was being a pain in my fucking ass like a hemorrhoid.

"Talk then Hassan. You want to talk so bad so talk!"

"I'm not saying anything until I know you're open to listening to what I have to say. Give me the same respect I've given you."

"Respect? You want to talk about respect? Did you respect me when you were fuckin' me knowing you had a girlfriend? Huh, Hassan? Did you?"

"You never asked," he responded sounding stupid.

"I never asked? How about you're supposed to tell bitches that up front. Or how about you don't try pursuing anyone knowing you have ties to the next bitch. I shouldn't have to ask. You knew you had a girlfriend!"

"And you knew there was somebody in the picture. Come on Satin, you don't peg me as dumb. The first time we saw each other I had a girl with me. Use your brain ma."

"I'm not a fuckin' mind reader for one. For two are we done here? You're really killing my buzz," I told him as I finally picked myself up off the floor,taking a seat on my bed.

"You serious right now?"

"As fuck. Your dick good and all but it ain't all that. I can do without the extra shit. I mean it ain't like we were together or no shit like that anyways."

"You heard what you just said, right? We weren't together. You trippin' for what beautiful? I withheld information. I never lied to you. I'm tryna explain but your mean ass won't let me."

"Fine Hassan. Explain!"

"The woman you heard in the background, she's uh she's one of my girlfriends."

"Wait, what? What you mean she's one of your girlfriends? What type of sick shit is this?" I asked him as I scrunched my face up.

"I'm a polyamorist. I believe in multiple partners. It's my lifestyle. So yes technically I'm in a relationship with multiple women. No, they're not all the same and that's what makes this shit dope. Every single one of them are unique and offer something different. For so long I thought-," he tried to continue to explain but I had to cut him off.

I was hearing everything he was saying but I still was baffled by it all. He had some serious issues if he thought this shit was normal. It just seems weird. Like who just goes around dating multiple people? And what bitch alive is okay with it knowingly?

"And you was trying to involve me in this weird shit? How many of them are they and don't lie!"

"Three but I wasn't trying to involve you. I took one look at you and I instantly wanted you. I wanted to know you. Wanted to know what your insides felt like. How soft your lips would feel against mine. I just wanted you and I'll admit I was being selfish but I couldn't just pass you up."

"Leave. Please. I don't even know why you brought your ass up here anyways. You wasted your time. I want nothing to do with you. With any of this ass backwards shit, you have going on. Let's call it even. You got some pussy and I got some dick. I think it's safe to say we both got what we wanted," I told him as I looked into his face.

"Satin.. Just, just listen to me," he begged sounding desperate but I didn't need to hear anything else. I was good. Shit wasn't that deep between the two of us anyways.

"I heard enough. You can leave though."

"You serious? You really just gonna kick me out?"

"Hassan just go. This conversation is done. You really did waste your time flying all the way up here."

"Say no more then. You know? I could make you a very happy woman but it seems like you already made your choice," he said as he walked out of my bedroom and out of the front door.

I ain't have shit to say to Hassan. Like what was I supposed to say to that bomb he dropped on me? I couldn't for the life of me understand his way of thinking or his lifestyle as he put it. Ain't no way in hell Ima be cool with a nigga having extra-curricular activities. Nope. I'm not the bitch for that. He could miss me all the way with it.

Isabella

As I moved around my kitchen preparing to cook breakfast for Sincere and me, I couldn't help but think about everything that happened yesterday. I couldn't believe Kori and her actions. I know I shouldn't be surprised because she was always messing around with somebody's husband however, I thought she had more class then that. She could've had an affair with anybody else's husband in this city. Why did she have to fool around with our friend husband? None of it was making sense.

The entire time she kept mentioning her *'boo'* she was referring to Jacob's cheating ass the whole damn time. Honestly, though, I'm not surprised that Jacob even violated in that way because let's be honest here. He's a man and a man gonna catch whatever you throw his way. Now that I think about it I need to ask Sin if the brown skin girl he saw Jacob with was Kori and how come he didn't mention that detail.

Adding blueberries to my pancake batter I swayed my tiny hips to Bruno Mars and Cardi B's new song Finesse as I felt a pair of arms wrap around my waist and I instantly smiled.

"Good morning my love," I cooed as my soon to be husband kissed my neck.

"Good morning baby. You got it smelling good in here. What's the occasion?" he asked me as he snatched a piece of bacon off the platter that was sitting on the counter.

"No occasion, I just wanted to do something nice for you. I've been so busy with work and then you know I got in late last night from Joi's, so I wanted to spend some time with you and maybe talk about wedding plans."

"Speaking of Joi, how is she holding up?"

"She's good. We got her settled in after she was discharged from the hospital but you know things wouldn't be right if there wasn't any drama involved."

"What happened?" he asked taking a seat at our breakfast bar pouring a glass of orange juice from the pitcher I had sitting there.

"Well," I started to say with a long drawn out sigh.

"Dream, Satin and I helped Joi into the house and all hell broke loose. Joi found Jacob in bed with another woman."

"What? Nah my man's ain't that wild."

"Let me finishhh, guess who the woman was though."

"Who?"

"Kori!"

"Your friend Kori? The dude?" he asked choking on his juice.

"You playin' right?"

"I'm dead serious. He's been cheating with Kori. I'm so baffled. I don't even know how to process it. I just feel so bad for Joi. That type of betrayal will have me ready to murk somebody," I told him as I put some pancakes on his plate.

"Baby you ain't tough. But that's some spicy talk. Did he know that uh you know Kori was born a boy?"

"Nope. She never told him. I told her before about that. She just be trickin' these dudes and one day one of these niggas gonna choke her ass."

"What did ol' girl say about all of this?"

"She didn't say much. I think she was in a state of shock. She kicked us out. I've been tryna call her but she hasn't answered or responded to any of my text messages," I stated in a defeated tone.

"Give her some space. I know you don't want to but ya girl is hurtin' and she probably just embarrassed. She'll come around just don't be so overbearing."

"I guess you're right. I just don't want her to think she has to deal with any of this mess on her own, you know? We're her girls so I want her to know we got her back all the way."

"I hear you Bella but give her some space. Aight?"

"Fine. I'll try to."

"No, you will. I know you, Isabella. You always in somebody's business tryna fix shit. Let people go through what they have to go through. Just be there for her when she's ready," he told me and I walked over and placed my arms around his neck.

I was so blessed to have a man like Sincere. He knew what to say and when to say it. Looking into his brown eyes I couldn't help but feel like the luckiest girl in the world and instantly that Destiny's Child song came to mind and I smiled before I began singing to him.

"I'm so happy, so happy that you're in my life and baby now that you're apart of me you show me, show me the true meaning of loveee," I sung before placing a soft kiss on his lips.

"That's how you feelin'?" he asked as he took his hands and rubbed on my booty.

"Always baby."

"You ridin' with me?"

"Always and forever."

"That's what the fuck I'm talkin' bout. I love your ass, Bella."

"I love you too Sin," I replied back to him through a smile.

****

"Satin!" Dream yelled as we entered the house. Satin ass lives slap dab in the middle of the hood and her front door was unlocked and that ain't like her. Dream and I both tried callin' this girl multiple times and neither one of us was able to get ahold of her so after I finished with Sincere I met Dream here.

"Saaatiiinnnnnn," I sung out but still got no response as we finally made it to her bedroom where she was knocked out in bed.

"Wake up hoe!" Dream demanded as she snatched the covers back.

"Dream leave me alone. I feel like shit," Satin whined.

"You look like shit too. Get yo ass up and wash your ass so we can talk."

"I don't feel good. Let me just stay hereee."

"Satin, seriously? Get up. Why don't you feel good all of a sudden?"

"She's hungover. Look at her," I said with a giggle.

"I just want to know who she was drinkin' with and why weren't we invited."

"Ughh my fuckin' head hurts. Please just let me lay here," she pouted.

"Has Kori been here?" Dream asked as she removed her shoes and got in the bed with Satin as I took a seat in her chair.

"Not since I've been here."

"Did you know?"

"Did I know what?" Satin asked after she swallowed two pills, I'm assuming for her headache.

"That Kori was fuckin' Jacob," Dream responded.

"Dream? Really?" I questioned.

"What? It's just a question. That is her cousin."

"So you think I'd keep a secret like that from one of my best friends? Really Dream? You think I'm that fucked up?"

"I'm just sayin Satin, y'all live together how didn't you know?"

"What Kori does isn't any of my business. I didn't know she was fuckin' him. In case you didn't notice I was just as shocked as the three of you. I had no idea that's who her so-called boo was. Had I known I would've stopped the shit before it even started," she said and I believed her. Satin wasn't that type of girl so I was honestly blown that Dream out of all people would even come at her like that.

"Alright Satin. You don't have to get all sensitive. I was just asking a question."

"Bitch, you just accused me of some real foul shit. How was I not supposed to get offended? You know me Dream. You know I don't even be on that type of time."

"My bad Sat, damn. What's really your issue? You clearly feeling some type of way."

"Nothing," Satin said with a deep sigh.

"I came home last night and Hassan's foreign ass was here in my bedroom."

"Okay. Why is that a bad thing?" I asked.

"Because I don't want nothing to do with him. I told y'all that. He lied. I'm not with that lying shit. Granted he offered to pay for me to go to hair school but at this point, I can't fake shit with him just to get what I want. The nigga is a dog."

"You still salty about the girlfriend thing?" Dream asked her.

"Y'all don't even know the half of it. Let's just say he's not who I thought he was."

"Aww, my baby fell for him. Satin got under some new dick and got dick whipped now she in her feelings."

"Dream.. Shut up. Please."

"It's true though."

"Anyone try gettin in touch with Joi?" I asked them changing the subject.

"Nope, she sent my calls to voicemails. Petty heffa," Dream said with an attitude.

"I tried a couple of times last night but got nothing. I hope she's okay," Satin added.

"Y'all tryna go to her house?" I asked them and Dream looked at me like I was crazy.

"Bitch is you crazy? She don't want to be bothered obviously. Give it a couple of days," Dream said to me and I rolled my eyes. I don't care what Sincere and Dream was talkin' about. My friend was hurting and she was temporarily handicapped. I wasn't leaving shit alone.

Joi

Tell me how did we end up this way, never miss a good

thing til it's gone away. Sittin' here trying to reason with

myself when you were thinkin' about someone else.

Sayin' sorry won't take away the pain. Seems we'll never

ever be the same cause I was your everything and you

were my everything.. Where do I go from hereee?

Words couldn't express how I was feeling right now. The pain that I felt was so unbearable and I just wanted it to go away. It hurt more than the foot injury I currently had. How could he? How could she? Two people, I loved more than myself betrayed me in a way that I never could have imagined.

I was more hurt than I was angry. Does that make sense to you? For the life of me, I couldn't wrap my head around this situation. Like what would make either one of them think sleeping with each other behind my back was okay? Or better yet how did Kori think shit was sweet with her admitting in front of me that she loved him? I felt like I was in a twilight zone when those words escaped her lips. Like it wasn't real.

I know I shouldn't have been surprised by Jacob's actions but truthfully I was. Him having relations with Kori was a low blow. Yeah, he's cheated plenty of times before but never with anyone close to me. This was a tough pill to swallow. And I can't imagine forgiving either one of them. Like why would they do this to me? What did I do to deserve this?

Maybe it was my karma. Like Kori said I knew she had a thing for him but that was years ago. We were in high school and Kori couldn't come on to Jacob as she could now. Not once did I think she would be holding a grudge against me for marrying him. Or plotting on my man right in front of my face. When I got introduced to the new Kori not once did I think having her around Jacob would be an issue but as you can see I was wrong.

I was so embarrassed. Hurt. Confused. I've been laying in the same spot since I've came home yesterday. The only time I've gotten up was to use the bathroom and that wasn't often because I refused to eat or drink anything. I just wanted to be by myself and just be in my funk. I had Olivia's 'Where Do I Go?' song playing on repeat as I continuously cried to myself wondering why me. I was having a pity party for myself even though it was probably foolish.

To make matters worse Jacob kept calling me nonstop but I had nothing to say to him. I just wanted his dumbass to leave me alone. I wanted nothing to do with him. I forgave him time and time again and that's my fault because I kind of made his behavior okay. Even after he said he was willing to change and try to be the man I needed him to be he turned around and lied just to do this to me. I can no longer take that risk. He's bad for me. He's bad for my mental health.

I'm sure it'll be hard to start over but that's just something I'm going to have to do. 12 long years together and it was a waste. A waste of time. A waste of love. A waste of a relationship. Just a complete waste all the way around. I should've walked away a long time ago but it makes absolutely no sense to dwell on should've could've would've. It is what it is and things will be what they're going to be.

I just wanted this pain to go away. I wanted to fast forward to my happy ending, well that's if there is one. There had to be one, right? There's no way that I've gone through this much pain and hurt just to stay stuck here. There was life after my heartache. There just had to be.

****

"Oh Joi, honey you have to get up boo," Isabella mentioned to me as I layed in bed staring at the ceiling.

"Isabella leave me alone. Go awayyyyy," I groaned as she reached for my arm to attempt to get me up but I wouldn't budge.

"Joi, you need to get up! You probably been laying here all day. Get up!"

"I should've took your spare keys. Should've known you would pop up."

"Is that an attitude I sense? I'm not the problem here Joi nor am I the enemy. I'm trying to help you and I'll gladly leave after. But right now I just want to get you cleaned, okay? Just let me help you."

"Isabella.. I can't. I can't move. It hurts. It hurts so baddddd," I said as I began sobbing hard.

"Booooo," she dragged out as she got in the bed with me and just wrapped her arms around me.

"I'm so sorry that you're even going through this. I swear I am."

"I don't understand. I don't understand how they could do this to meee. How, how could they be so cruel?"

"Fuck them. Joi, you're an amazing woman and Jacob, excuse my language has been an ain't shit nigga for fucking years. You deserve better than this. Better than him. Any man would be happy to have you by his side. As far as Kori if you like we can kick her ass and if Satin jumps in we can beat hers too," she said and I managed to let a small laugh escape my lips.

"Izzy you can't fight."

"And? That ain't stoppin me from trying to if you tryna get into some shit. I got ya back, baby."

"I don't know what I would do without you. Thank you for always being there. Seriously. I appreciate you, you have no idea."

"Girl you ain't gotta thank me for doing what friends do. I genuinely wish that I could take your hurt away but you have to go through this to get to where you're supposed to be. It won't be today, hell it probably won't be two months from now but you will get through this. Watch. "

"I love you, friend," I told her sincerely.

"You already know I love you too. Now, will you get up so I can help you clean your funky ass? I'll order some food and we can just chill out here all day. I'll call Sincere and let him know I won't be home til late," she suggested.

"Sounds good," I replied back as we let each other go preparing to get up.

I'm not even surprised Izzy stopped by. I expected her to. She has this nagging way of barging into other people lives even when you don't want to be bothered. In a way it was cute. My lil baby was as sweet as pie and I welcomed her company. I needed the distraction for now.

Kori

I've been trying to call Jacob every since he stormed out of Joi's house but he had blocked me. I couldn't let him go without him hearing me out first. I know I lied but I lied for a very good reason. Jacob was supposed to be mine and Joi stole him from me. It started when we were all in high school. You see Jacob, Joi and I all graduated in the same class. I saw Jacob first and Joi knew I wanted him. She knew I had a crush on him but because I was a boy I couldn't let those feelings be known so I just admired him from a distance.

After high school, I picked up and moved to Atlanta for a few years where I transitioned into a female. I always knew I was gay. I always thought I was supposed to be a woman and I made a vow that when I was old enough I would become one and as you can see, I did just that. The whole process was long and very expensive and once I started there was no turning back.

From hormone pills, injections, breast and ass implants and a reassignment surgery I knew I was going to need plenty of money to become the woman I knew I deserved to be so I became a male escort. Thankfully I was an escort for the wealthy and was able to speed up the process and had a few of my sponsors pay for what needed to be done. Long story short once I was satisfied with what I looked liked I moved back home to Springfield and I was a whole new person. Hell, even my own cousin didn't recognize me.

Nobody understood what it felt like growing up wishing you were somebody else. I was meant to be a woman. Call me crazy but I really believed I was born the wrong gender. I would play in my grandmother's makeup when I was younger and it always led to me getting a beating but every one of those beatings were worth it to me. She used to call me a faggot and even tried to send me to Gender Conversion Therapy yet nothing worked. I still felt how I felt and I hated her for that. I still do which is why I didn't care about her slipping into a damn coma. Her old ass deserved it.

Anyways once I moved back I got reconnected with Joi and saw that she had married the love of my life and my heart broke. He was supposed to be mine, luckily for me, he didn't recognize me and Joi never brought up my old life. Neither did Satin. They accepted this *new* Kori with open arms. I felt like I had a new chance at life and that I could finally have a chance with Jacob.

I know it's shady but I was plotting on Jacob the moment I stepped foot on Springfield's soil. I didn't care who I had to hurt in the process. I was going to have everything I wanted at any cost and unfortunately, Joi was in the way. You see I didn't want to do it but she knew how I felt. If nobody else did, she did. She knew he was off limits. She fucking knew.

I just hate that Satin got tangled in my bullshit. I know it doesn't seem like it but I have a soft spot for her. Satin and I bond is deeper than one could possibly think. She always had my back and I've always looked out for her. I felt like it was my job since the day she came home from the hospital. I actually thought about writing her a letter letting her know that I'm sorry. I can't bring myself to see her. And even though I should've been worried about Joi and me friendship I didn't care about it. I was more concerned with Satin.

Picking up my phone I threw it against the wall and released a loud scream. I didn't know what to do. I couldn't go back home. I couldn't face my friends. I needed to see Jacob. I need him to know we could still be together. I was still the Kori he fell for, just now he knows my secret. A secret I was tired of hiding.

Jacob loved me. He would forgive me, right? I mean he had to when he calmed down. He had to. Life isn't worth living if I couldn't be with him. He was meant for me. I was meant for him. He was my soulmate. I know I hurt him but it wasn't my intentions too. I would've eventually told him. Well maybe. I don't know. I don't know what I'm saying. I'm just rambling. I don't know what more to do. I'm living a fucking nightmare.

"UGHHHHHHHHHHHHHHHHHHHHH," I screamed out loud as I pulled on my own hair as I rocked back and forth. Jacob was going to be mine. He had to be whether he wanted to be or not.

Dream

"You feeling better boo?" I asked Satin as we layed in her bed watchin Wild'n Out on MTV.

"Yeah finally. I swear I'm never drinking again. I don't know who said I was even grown. Out here mixing mad shit."

"So you gonna tell me what's bothering you or am I gonna have to drag it out of you? It's just the two of us and I know you Sat. I know you better than you know yourself."

"I'm good Dream. I just been doing a lot of thinking lately. My life needs a change. I look around at you all and y'all are all established in y'all careers meanwhile I feel like I'm not doing shit," she admitted.

"What you mean you ain't doing shit? Satin as long as I've known you, you've been slaying the fuck outta some hair and taking care of your grandmother. Girl that ain't nothing. You're talented and you're caring. Not to mention one of the realest bitches I've ever met."

"But Dream, I still don't have a career. My grandmother is more than likely not coming home and I can't work in anybody's shop because I don't even have my cosmetology license. So again, I'm not doing shit."

"Everything you just said you can do something about it. Your grandmother may not be coming home so you need to find out what it is Satin is passionate about. Find something that you're going to love to do forever and turn it into a career. Bitch open up your own shop. You can do anything."

"Yeah, with what money? I'm not tryna go into debt."

"I can loan it to you. I'm not balling or no shit like that but if you're really tryna go to hair school then I'll help. Besides Mega gives me more than enough money then I know what to do with," I told her sincerely.

I wasn't used to this side of Satin. She's always the strong one. Carefree. Loving. Outgoing one but looking at her now, has me looking at her differently. Not differently in a bad way or no shit like that but it's a softer side that I'm not used to seeing.

"Speaking of Mega, what's going on with y'all?" she asked me and I sucked my teeth.

"Girl, I don't even know. He still out in New York. I'm tryna be patient and see where shit gonna go with the two of us but you know me. You know I'm not really into the relationship thing. I like him though, don't get me wrong but he moving funny."

"What you mean?"

"I don't know. Like he just don't feel as interested as he was in the beginning. I mean it could just be me though. You know I stay looking for a reason not to fuck with a nigga. Plus the nigga been out of town for how long?"

"Maybe he's just busy Dream. You know you're the queen of overthinking."

"Says the girl who googles everything when something isn't normal to her," I joked back to her.

"Hey, some shit don't be normal. Oh wassup with ya other boo thang?"

"Bitch don't start. You know damn well."

"What? What I say?" she asked through a giggle. "She is your boo. You just don't know it yet."

"I see you got jokes. I'm not gay Satin, stop playing with me."

"You don't have to be gay to kiss another girl. You can just be curious. Admit it Dream you're curious. It's okay."

Was I curious? Or did I just enjoy the attention Sosa gave me? I mean she's so cool. We vibe so well and I forget that she's even a woman until we're in each others space. I wasn't sure what I was feeling. I've looked at other girls but never have I've ever been interested in one. This thing with Sosa had me confused as fuck.

I don't even know why I had to put a label on my sexuality. Why couldn't I just like who I like and call it a day? Why did I have to put a label to it? For other people? To get their approval so that they can put me in a box with others? I mean that's what it seems like.

"Maybe I am just a little curious," I said to Satin as I sat up in bed.

"But why do I have to put a label on it? Huh?"

"I don't know. That's just the way things are I guess," she said looking at me confused.

"But why are things this way? Have you ever asked yourself who made up all these rules and regulations? Why we're forced to categorize ourselves?"

"Dream.. I wasn't tryna turn it into a debate. I was just asking. Sheesh," she said and I didn't respond I just sat there in deep thought.

Was I straight? Bisexual? Bicurious? Who knows but I know I liked both Mega and Sosa. Society would only accept Mega and me because that's what a 'couple' consisted of. I know we're in a new day and age but same-sex relationships are still frowned upon. In a perfect world, I'd have both Sosa and Mega together. They both brought out different sides to me and I loved it. If only I could have that perfect three-way relationship. I can picture it now. The perfect fantasy.

I've always been the type to beat to my own drum and that's what I was going to continue to do. I was gonna do what Dream wanted to do with no regrets.

****

"Who is it?" I called out as I walked towards my apartment door. It was a little after 2 am so who the hell could be knocking at my door.

"Who is it?" I said again looking through the peephole and I saw a black figure. Against my better judgment, I opened my door and a shocked expression is what graced my face followed by anger.

"I need your help," Kori said to me and still, I just looked at her debating whether or not I should jump on her ass for that foul shit she pulled.

"No, what you need to do is go away. Bye Kori," I told her as I tried closing the door but she put her foot in the door stopping me.

"Dream just listen to me for a sec. Take this. Please. Give it to Satin for me," she said to me as she handed me an envelope.

"What's this?" I asked her.

"Just give it to her for me, okay? Please. That's all I'm asking. Just do this favor for me please," she said and I nodded my head to say yes and with that, she was gone.

That was weird. I thought to myself as I turned around and prepared to close my door but it was stopped before closing and caused me to stop in my tracks and turn back around to be met face to face with Mega.

"Act like you happy to see a nigga," he said as he gave me a cocky smirk.

"I would if I was actually happy. What are you doing here? Don't you have business to tend to in 'New York'," I told him in a sarcastic voice making sure to emphasize on New York.

"My business is done there. At least for now. So wassup? You gonna invite me in or ya other nigga here?"

"You fishin' for information. Cute. You can come in just don't think I'm giving you any pussy."

"Who said I wanted your little funky box? I just wanted to be up under you. Can I do that?" he asked me as he stepped closer to me staring in my eyes. I had to look away quickly before I got lost in his hazel eyes.

"You lucky I'm in the mood to cuddle or else I wouldn't let your ugly ass in," I told him as I turned around quickly to hide the small smile that was on my face.

"There's some leftovers in the fridge if you're hungry. I was on my way to bed before I started getting unexpected visitors"

"I'm not hungry, thanks for offering though. Let's go to bed. I haven't gotten a good night rest since the last time I saw you and right now all I'm tryna do is feel your smooth ass against me."

"I'm serious Mega, no sex!"

"Dreamy, baby.. I ain't on that tonight. You got my word ma. Just lay with a nigga. That's all I need. That's all I want. I deal with a bunch of niggas daily. I need this estrogen right now. Don't fight me on this. Just be a niggas calm. Can you do that for me? Be my calm? Be my peace?"

"Fine!"

"Aight. Get rid of the attitude too. I'm here now. I ain't going nowhere. And if I do you coming with me," he spoke to me as he pulled me into him and I felt at home.

Having his big strong arms wrapped around me had me feeling like maybe I could do this relationship thing with him . Like maybe he was the one. The only reason I was in my feelings anyways right now is because he's been gone. Inhaling his Cartier Declaration cologne I rested my head on his chest before turning to face him.

This man was the epitome of my version of a good man. From what I've been shown he was nothing short of amazing and despite our little issues lately, I couldn't deny the fact that he was good to me. Even when I didn't deserve him to be. He didn't hurt me. He didn't misuse me. He didn't disrespect me, he was the complete opposite of what I was used to and maybe that's why I was having such a hard time allowing myself to enjoy him entirely. In the back of my mind, he was gonna fuck up. He was gonna show his true colors and it would prove that I had the right to handle him the way I've been handling him.

I was torn. I had Mega who was everything any woman would want but I also had a part of me that was curious about Sosa and I wouldn't feel liberated I guess until I experienced her. Does that make sense to you? I wanted Mega. I cared for Mega but Sosa, she was different. Our chemistry was different. I was conflicted. Very fuckin' conflicted.

Satin

I was finally feeling better so today I was going to the nursing home to see my baby. I missed my grandmother. Being in that big house alone just didn't feel right. As much as I wanted to have her discharged, I knew it was in her best interest to stay there so she could get the proper care she needed. I also felt like shit for missing out on visiting her for a couple of days.

Applying some mascara and eyeliner to my eyes I looked at myself in the mirror and threw my hair in a messy ponytail. I only had one thing on my agenda today and that was to see my nana so getting dolled up wasn't even necessary. Besides, I woke up feeling funny. I couldn't describe the feeling, I just felt weird. Felt off.

Grabbing my things I made my way out the door and got into the Uber that was waiting on me and I was on my way. Still, I couldn't shake the feeling I was having. Something wasn't right. What? I couldn't tell you but something in my spirit was telling me shit was all bad and I began getting nervous. As soon as we made it to the place that she was staying at I said a quick prayer to myself before getting out of the car.

As soon as I made it to my grandmother's room I breathed a sigh of relief as I saw her sitting up in bed. Her hair was done in a ponytail while she watched the TV that was in front of her. She was so into whatever she was watching that she didn't even notice me standing there.

"Hey beautiful," I greeted her with a smile walking further into the room.

"Oh hey baby, I see you finally decided to come see your old lady," she spoke to me giving me a bright smile.

"Now you know I couldn't stay away from you for too long. How are you doing? Feeling okay?"

"I'm as good as I could possibly be. You doing alright?"

"I'm good grandma. I'm still alive so I can't really complain," I told her as I took a seat in a chair that was next to her bed. Luckily she was in a private room.

"Now Satin, I know you. What's wrong? Talk to me. Give me the scoop as you young folks say."

"Grandma I'm good. I just miss you. I want you home."

"Baby, your grandma is old and you can't spend the rest of your life taking care of me. I'm okay Satin. I need you to be too. You worry too much."

"How can I not worry? You're all I have. I'll always be worried about you"

"There's something I've been wanting to talk to you about," she said in a serious tone with worry written all over her face and that made me nervous. Before I was able to respond a woman came into the room. She was beautiful. In fact, she was the replica of me. It was her. It was my mother.

"Hey momma," she greeted my grandmother before turning her attention to me.

"Satin, Oh baby I'm so happy to see you. Where have you-," she tried to say but I cut her off before she could finish.

"Been? That's what you were going to say right? Where have I been? I've been here taking care of your mother while mine has been out living life," I said with much attitude in my voice.

"Satin, just hear your mother out. She's sorry."

"Why? Why should I grandma? No disrespect but she's not my mother. You are. I don't know this woman and at almost 28 years of age I don't care to know her."

"Satin.."

"No grandma, you can forgive her but I won't. I don't have anything to say to her," I told my grandmother as I stood up. I hadn't even been there long but I was already over this visit.

"Satin! Sit your big ass down while I'm talking to you! I may be in this bed but you will respect me. Sit your ass down and listen to me," she demanded and I listened. I never went against my grandmother and I won't start now.

"Momma it's okay. I understand," my mother said with a sniffle.

"She hates me. I don't blame her."

"Renee hush up. We're not going to have some damn pity party. Both of y'all better listen up and hear me loud and clear. I am not going to live forever. My health is detreating and I need for you two to make amends. Satin I know that sounds impossible but she's your mother. She birthed you. She's the reason for your existence. You don't have to forget but baby girl you have to forgive. Life is about forgiving. Forgive her, not for her but for yourself. For your peace of mind," she said as she reached for my hand.

"Can you do that for me?"

"Yes," I told her just above a whisper.

"That's my girl. Now, Renee, she has every right to be mad at you. You abandoned her. You cannot make up for lost times so don't even try. Just try to be there for her now. She's going to need you. I can't have you two being estranged when I'm dead and gone. My soul won't rest until I know the two of you are okay. I forgave you and in due, to time she'll forgive you as well."

"Grandma why you talking like that?"

"Baby I just want to prepare you for what's to come. I want you to always be alright. I'm not gonna live forever. Go to school. Sell the house. Open that salon you've always said you wanted. Go be a phenomenal woman. Stop letting things hinder you from doing what it is you want to do, you hear me? Satin go be the best version of you possible."

"Nana!"

"Nana nothing. You heard what I said. Live your life, Satin. I lived mine. It's time for you to live yours."

"But grandmaaa."

"Stop that whining girl. Your grandmother is going to be alright. Stop worrying about me."

"I can't help it, I love you," I told her as tears fell from my eyes. I needed to get my shit together. She was right, I needed to go after what I said I've always wanted. Where there's a will there's a way and I was going to find a way.

As far as my mother is concerned, I don't have anything to say to her. She left me and let her mother do the job she should've been doing and I'll never forgive her for that. If you ask me she was a sorry excuse of a woman. Maybe one day we'll be able to get past this but today will not be the day. I know my grandmother meant well but I wasn't here for none of it.

"I love you too my Satin," she spoke to me softly.

****

Three days later

"Hey boo. Wassup?" I asked Dream as I walked up to the table she was sitting at and taking a seat. She called me and invited me to lunch.

"Hey, pretty girl, how you doing? Haven't heard from you these past few days."

"I'm alright, just taking care of business. I finally got a car."

"Bitchhhhh when?" Dream asked excitedly.

"Girl calm down it's a little hoopty. A 2006 Honda Accord. I needed something for right now. I was spending way too much on Ubers."

"Bitch bye. A car is a car. As long as it gets you from point A to point B, that's all that matters. And I don't even own a car. I'm still pushin Mega's shit."

"Speaking of which what's going on with y'all? I was at the registry the other day and some bird brain bitches was talkin' about some nigga that fit his description. They on his shit but from what was said he curved one of them," I told her as I laughed.

"As he fuckin' should. These hoes and their tired ass pussy better stay away from mine. They obviously don't know he fuckin' with me and I'm liable to kick one of their thot asses in the damn neck."

"You going hard for someone who claims to be single."

"I am single, he isn't though. He goes with me and I go well, with nobody. I'm having fun."

"Something is really wrong with you."

"Hey, you gotta beat them at their own game. Anyways I called you here to give you something," she told me as she dug in her purse and sliding me an envelope.

"What's this?"

"I don't know. The other night some weird shit happened. I was getting ready for bed and I heard knocks on my door. When I got to the door Kori was standing there. She looked crazy."

"Okay, what does that have to do with the envelope?"

"She told me to give it to you. I didn't open it. I didn't feel as though it was my place to."

"That just seems weird though. Why didn't she just give it to me? We live together. Wait she hasn't even been home. Her door has remained closed since the day we all left Joi's. What you think it is?"

"I don't know. Knowing Kori it's something dramatic. Probably something you shouldn't open in public. You never know with that one," Dream responded taking a sip of the margarita she had ordered.

"I guess. Have you been able to get in touch with Joi? I keep trying to call her but she won't answer."

"Same thing for me. I mean we know she's home let's just go by. You got a key, right?"

"Oh shit, I forgot all about my damn key. You're so right. Let's pop up. She's gonna talk to us one way or another," I told Dream as I got up.

"Ima stop by KFC and grab some food and I'll meet you there, cool?"

"We're already at a restaurant though Satin. Why would you do that?"

"Because I'm not eating here and I need my food to go, besides Ima, bring Joi some. Any more questions?"

"Don't get smart. Ima pay for this drink and head out. Get me something to eat too since we ain't eating here."

"You already know I was. You ain't even have to ask me. See you in a few."

"See you in few," she told me and we briefly parted ways. Joi couldn't ignore us forever. I understood she was going through something but she needed us, whether she wanted to admit it or not.

Joi

"Is that the last box?" I asked one of the movers I had removing Jacob's things from my house.

"Yes, ma'am. Do you need anything else?" he asked as he stopped and looked at me. He was a looker and if I wasn't in my current situation I'd definitely would be interested.

"No, I was just asking. Don't mind me."

"You sure you don't need anything else?"

"I'm positive," I told him as I heard Dream's voice.

"Actually we'll take your number if that's alright with you," she flirted and I think I saw him blush before he walked away.

"Dream!" I called out.

"What? He's cute. You get over one man by getting under another."

"I'm not going there with you today. What are you doing here?"

"Uh, I came to see my friend. I mean we are friends, right?"

"Friends? You sure that's what we are?" I asked her jokingly.

"Don't play with me. I know we don't always get along but you're still a friend of mine. Now friend why haven't you been answering our calls?"

"Ours?"

"Yes ours, bitch you haven't been answering mine either," Satin said with an attitude as she carried in some food from KFC.

"I haven't been in a social mood."

"But you were in the mood to pack up his shit? Who helped you? I know you didn't do all of this on your own with a messed up foot."

"If you must know Izzy stopped by the other day," I replied.

"Ohhh I get it Isabella is your only friend. Got it," Dream said as she and Satin headed to the kitchen.

"I never said that. Y'all know Isabella is overbearing. She popped up just like y'all irritating asses."

"Mmmmhmm," Satin responded back to me and I couldn't help but laugh a little. She was really mad.

"Satin don't be mad. You here now."

"Not the point heffa. We're your friends. We've been worried about you."

"I'm alright y'all. I'm a big girl. I'll be just fine."

"We know that you're going to be fine but right now you're not. You don't have to pretend for us," Dream tried to sympathize but I didn't want to talk about me. I didn't want to talk about that situation.

"I.. I just don't want to talk about it, alright? I appreciate y'all looking out and all but I just want to deal with it on my own. You guys understand that, right?" I asked and they nodded their heads yes although I knew they didn't.

This wasn't a typical breakup. This was a marriage. We exchanged vows. We were a union. Walking away isn't as easy when there's been time invested. I kept saying I had to figure a way out of my marriage and now that one has presented itself I'm finding myself questioning everything, myself included. It's like I didn't know myself outside of him. He's all I've known, all I've been about for the past decade-plus. So although my friends are trying to comfort me there's nothing anyone can do to help me through this process. I have to go through it on my own. I'm the one living this nightmare, not them.

Everyone always tries to offer sympathy when you're going through things and say 'I'm here if you need anything' but when all you need is a listening to ear that won't judge or shame you can you really confide in them? Can you really expect them to put themselves in your shoes and truly wholeheartedly sympathize with you. I may not be okay today but in time I will be.

"Sooooooo," Satin dragged out breaking the awkward silence," we gonna eat or what? I'm hungry."

"You're always hungry Satin," I said with a giggle.

"I feel like you just called me fat. Not cool Joi, not cool."

"You know you ain't fat baby. You thick!"

"With a whole lot of asssssss," Dream joined in sticking her tongue out like Cardi B.

"It is fat, huh?" she asked as she twerked a lil bit.

"Go bestfrannnnn!" Dream and I said at the exact same time and we both fell out in laughter.

"Y'all silly as hell."

"You started it, over here showing out. Twerking and shit. That's why that little cutie from Miami was stuck. What's his name again?" I asked and she rolled her eyes.

"Hassannnnnnn," Dream sung out.

"Girl boo. Ain't nobody thinking about him."

"Satin why you playin? You know you miss that man. Y'all look good together. I say you fuck him one last time."

"Excuse me?"

"You heard me! Fuck. Him. One. Last. Time! You know you want to and I honestly don't blame you. Foreign dick must be good, had yo ass all in yo feelings."

"Dream shut up! Wasn't nobody in their feelings, okay? I was mad that he lied."

"Lies! You don't have to lie to us Sat, we know the real. You fell for him," Dream stated

"Sure did," I cosigned.

"I didn't fall for him. I just enjoyed the sex," she tried to say but I knew better. Satin liked the man.

"Anywayssss Joi, can I be real with you for a minute?" she asked in a serious tone.

"Satin," I started off saying because I already knew where this conversation was heading.

"Just hear me out. I just want you to know that I had no idea what was going on. I swear to you. I don't want you thinking I knew what was up when I really didn't."

"I'm not even gonna lie and say that the thought never crossed my mind because it did but then I remembered that I knew you. I know that you're not some fucked up ass person."

"So, you're not mad at me?"

"Be mad at you for what? You can't control what Kori does with her boy pussy. She's her own person. I will tread lightly with what comes out of my mouth because at the end of the day she's your cousin and you're going to have her back."

"You're right, she is my cousin. However wrong is wrong and right is right. I'm with you when you right but when you wrong I want no parts of it. I can't have her back with this one, so you are entitled to feel anyway that you feel. I just don't want this situation to come in between our friendship we managed to build. That's all."

"And it won't unless you let it."

"Ugh y'all so damn mushy," Dream said as she pulled out a bottle of tequila out of her purse pouring some in her cup.

"Bitch did you just pull out a whole bottle out your bag?"

"Yes, yes I did. Y'all was killing my little buzz I had going on. I need it to come back. Over here having a kumbaya moment and shit."

"What is wrong with you?" I asked her laughing.

"She's a damn nut, that's what's wrong with her."

"Y'all gonna keep talking shit or y'all gon partake in some day drinking with me?"

"I want no parts of that. Nope. I was sick for a whole fucking day. Alcohol is not my friend. The older I get the harder it is to get over a hangover. I'm all set," Satin replied to Dream.

"I'm on crutches so Issa no for me. You enjoy that boo."

I may not be in the best of spirits but at least I got my girls.

Dream

Two Weeks Later

"Mega, can you take this damn blindfold off of me now? I feel like I've been walking forever," I complained as he held my hands guiding me to some unknown destination.

"Dream, not even tryna be on some funny shit but learn to shut the fuck up sometimes. Ya man got you. Relax ma," he said and it just irritated me more than I already was.

"My man? Hmph. Some man you are. Tell me where you're bringing me. You know black girls don't do surprises."

"You know you really get on my nerves. Shit can never be smooth with you. You make everything complicated."

"Wouldn't be me if I didn't."

"Spoiled ass!"

"Says the man who spoils me."

"Spoil these nuts!" he joked and I tried to kick him and almost lost my balance but he made sure he caught me before I was even able to attempt to fall.

"Look at you, bouta break ya neck tryna be violent and shit."

"Megaaaa where are we going," I asked just as I heard

"SURPRISEEEEEEEEEEEE!"

Uncovering my eyes I stood in what looked to be a small private dining room with my friends and a couple of other people I held near and dear to my heart. I felt so special. Just looking around at the pink, white and gold decorations that read 'Happy Birthday' had me in tears. For the first time in a long time in my life, a birthday meant something to me.

I've been so used to spending my birthdays alone that they don't even mean anything anymore. Yeah, I have my friends but it seemed like everyone was off doing their own thing dealing with their own issues. Nobody even mentioned my birthday and me being the person that I am, I just didn't want to impose on them so seeing that Mega went out of his way to make my day special had me grinning from ear to ear.

"I can't believe you did all of this for me," I spoke to him softly as I gazed into his eyes.

"You know I got you Dreamy. I couldn't miss your big day. It's all about you," he responded back to me and I couldn't help but continue to smile up at him. I believed him. He's been nothing but amazing to me.

"Happy birthday bitchhhhhhhhhh!" Satin yelled as she walked up to me, moving Mega out of the way to give me a hug as Isabella and Joi followed behind her.

"Thank you with your drunk ass," I said with a giggle.

"Hey, it's an open bar. I'm taking full advantage."

"Happy birthday beautiful," Isabella said to me as she handed me a gift bag.

"Awww thank you. You didn't have to get me anything."

"Girl Bye. It's your birthday. I wasn't coming empty handed. Hell, I even dragged Sincere ass out with me. It's a celebration."

"I appreciate it. You have no idea how much this means to me. I swear. You and the girls are really my family," I began saying as a tear fell from my eye.

I couldn't help it. I know today was supposed to be a happy day but I couldn't help but shed a couple of tears. Every since my momma passed when I was fourteen I pretty much been on my own. I bounced around from family members houses but as soon as they got tired of me I was out on the streets again. These girls despite everything we go through they never left me.

I never got over my mother's passing and I probably never will. I mean it's kind of hard not to when your father was the reason for her being dead in the first place. I'll never forget it. It was my fourteenth birthday and we were on our way to celebrate and I can't remember exactly what happened but I know that my father asked my mother about some man and next thing you know all hell broke loose. He ran us straight into this guardrail on the highway and we ended up in a ditch as our car flipped over. All I remember was waking up in the hospital as a social worker had a somber look on her face. She told me my mother was dead.

Can you imagine how it feels to lose your mother on what's supposed to be your special day? I've never recovered from that. That day I lost my mother and father. My mother's sister took me in for a while but she had her own children to raise and having an extra mouth to feed was more than she could handle, so I stayed with any family members that would have me until I got tired and turned to the streets.

What I wouldn't give to hear my mother's voice again. Or see her wide bright smile. I wish I could tell her that I loved her and she would tell me she loved me too. I know her spirit is always around me and that's comforting but on days like today, I'm reminded of that night so when Mega surprised me with this I was in awe.

"Don't cry pooh," Isabella said as she consoled me.

"I'm just. I don't know. I'm just emotional," I told her as I tried fanning my eyes to keep the tears from falling again.

"She's proud of you," Joi smiled as she gave me a hug.

"Trust me. We don't always see eye to eye but I'm here if you need a shoulder. I know today is tough."

"Dream.. You don't look cute crying and you're messing up your makeup," Satin spoke as she dapped at my face.

"Come on, let's go get you a drink."

"Satin you need to stay away from the bar," Joi told her as she rolled her eyes.

"Uh no, you need to mind your business and get you a drink and stay out of mine. Me drinking ain't bothering you."

"It is when it's only about to be 8 o'clock and you're almost drunk. Slow down a lil bit."

"Again, mind your business Joi and take a chill pill. I'm grown."

"Whatever Satin," Joi said with an attitude as she limped away. I couldn't wait til she took that damn walking boot off. Ugly ass thing looked like a moon boot.

As Satin and I made our way to the bar I looked around the room and everyone was smiling and mingling with one another. Mega did good. The place was decorated beautifully and the DJ was rockin'. As my eyes continued to scan the room they finally found Mega's and he winked an eye at me before turning his attention back to a dude I never seen before.

Ordering a Long Island, I slowly sipped on my drink before asking Satin a question.

"You talk to Hassan?"

"Have you spoken to your girlfriend?" Satin shot back at me and I turned red in embarrassment.

"That's not my girlfriend. I wish you'd stop calling her that."

"Why? You be spending time with her like she's your girlfriend."

"I really don't. Since Mega has been back, I've only texted her here and there. I'm starting to feel bad. Especially now after he did this."

"As you should. You know Mega worships the ground you walk on. I don't know why you even thought it was okay to entertain somebody else. A woman who wants to be a man at that."

"Shut up Satin. I don't know what Mega be doing when he's not around me. The nigga was in New York for how long?"

"Doesn't matter. He was coming to see you in between time. That has to count for something. I like him for you. If any nigga deserves a fair chance it's him. Give it to him Dream."

"You should try taking our own advice, you know that? Hassan isn't that bad of a guy either."

"That's where you're wrong. Did you forget that his lame ass has multiple girlfriends? I don't have time for none of that!"

"Who gives a fuck about those other bitches? Them hoes ain't you. He clearly wasn't thinking about them if he was chasing behind your ass."

"Not the point."

"Yes, it is. Satin you playing right now. That man wants you. Hell, even a blind man can see that. The nigga gasses up his jet to come and see you. You got him in his feelings and it's obvious he has you in yours."

"I'm not in my feelings. I'm just not about to let him do whatever his punk ass thinks he can do. Nah not me. Fuck him."

"Too late. You did that already and that's why your ass is acting all stank," I told her.

Satin is forever tryna give somebody some advice but for once she needs to take her own. She knows good and damn well she likes Hassan and it's obvious he likes her ass too. She can stand here and act like she some heartless bitch and haven't caught feelings if she wants to but I know the real. I know her. Hell, I probably knew her better than she knows herself.

If I believed that she truly didn't want anything to do with him I wouldn't even keep bringing it up but I knew better.

Satin

I was getting tired of Dream telling me that I liked Hassan more than I led on. Don't get me wrong he was cool and all but I wasn't all heartbroken and shit over what happened. He lied, therefore, I had every right to cut him off. I don't know how she expects me to just be all cool with what he did because if it was the other way around and I did the same shit to him he would've called me everything but my name and went on about his business.

Yes, we live in a man's world but why can't we switch it up? Every time you turn around women are always being so forgiven and nonchalant all for some selfish ass man to come along and take advantage. I wasn't with it anymore. If and that's a strong if I decided to fuck with Hassan again it'll be on my terms. Not his or anyone else's for that matter.

"Dream," I sighed as I put my empty cup down unto the bar.

"Don't worry about Hassan and I. Okay?"

"Satin I just want you happy. He was doing that," she spoke back to me with a half smile.

"A man can't make me happy, he can add to it but ultimately it's my decision. I'm going to be happy because I'm going to make sure that I am. Trust me I'm good Dream."

"You didn't have to get all technical on me. I'm just saying no man is perfect and they all aren't Rob. You may potentially be blocking your own happiness."

"Says the girl who has a great guy yet wants some pussy. Okay Dream," I laughed as I walked away from her leaving her at the bar.

I wasn't thinking about Dream or the stuff she was saying. I wasn't settling for a piece of a man just to say I have one because that's exactly what I'd be doing if I gave in to Hassan. So nah, I rather stay single and work on becoming a better me. Besides I got enough shit going on in my life and truthfully I need not to add anything else.

Making my way over to Joi I took a seat next to her and just placed my hand on top of hers giving it a nice squeeze. Things have been a little weird every since it came out that Kori was having an affair with Jacob. I know she said that situation wouldn't interfere with our friendship but I couldn't help but think that it semi did. It can be me and my usual over thinking self but it seems like every time I called she wouldn't answer my calls. Not to mention I haven't seen her since the last time Dream and I did the pop-up.

I may have met Joi through Kori but I truly did consider her one of my good friends. She was always so loving and there when I needed her to be. She as well as Izzy were two of the kindest and sweetest women I have ever met and I'd hate for anything to come in between us. And speaking of Kori nobody has heard or seen her. It's like she disappeared or something.

"Hey," I said just above a whisper as my voice cracked.

"Hey beautiful girl," Joi responded back as she wore her signature smile.

"I love you."

"I love you too Satin. You know that."

"Always?"

"Always."

"You've been okay? You know considering everything?" I questioned and still, she smiled only this time it didn't have that brightness behind it. It was dull.

"Now is not the time or place for that topic Sat. You understand that, right?"

"Of course. Say no more."

"Thank you. Now let's enjoy this party," she said and just like that the conversation ended.

I wasn't going to ask Joi anything else regarding her marriage. In fact, I wouldn't even bring up the situation at all. It was for her to deal with and I could only do my part as a friend as long as she allowed me to.

****

I know you're thinking I'm heartless. I know you're thinking I'm cold.

I'm just protectin' my innocence. I'm just protectin' my soul.

I'm never gonna let you close to me even though you mean the most to

me. Cause every time I open up it hurts. So I'm never gonna get too

close to you even when I mean the most to you, in case you go and

leave me in the dirt. But every time you hurt me the less that I cry.

And every time you leave me the quicker these tears dry. And

every time you walk out the less I love you. Baby, we don't stand a chance, it's sad but it's true. I'm way too good at goodbyes.

I was currently playing Sam Smith's 'Too Good At Goodbye' as I cleaned up the house. I wanted to thoroughly clean everything and get rid of some stuff seeing as though I'm pretty much the only one living here. This house was way too big and a lot of things we've accumulated over the years could go. As I started clearing things off the kitchen counter I came across the envelope Dream had given me. I had forgotten all about. As I got ready to open it there were knocks at the front door causing me to place it back down.

Making my way to the door and opening I came face to face with Renee. My mother. Rolling my eyes I turned and walked away and left her standing in the doorway. I wasn't in the mood for her sob stories. She wanted a pity party and I wasn't the one who was going to give it to her.

"You coming in or are you just going to stand there looking stupid?" I asked with my back towards her.

"I'm sure my mother taught you better than that," she said in a dry voice as her heels clicked against the tile. Once she made it to where I was in the kitchen I took a deep breath and finally turned around to look at her.

"What can I do you for Renee?"

"We need to talk."

"About?"

"Why I left you and how we can get past it."

"Get past it? How do you suppose we get past it? You say things like that when people cheat. Not when you've abandoned your own child!"

"I'm not perfect Satin. I've made mistakes but you will not continue to hold them against me. I was young. I knew nothing of being a mother. I was just a baby myself. I did what I felt was right."

"Leaving me with your mother was the only solution? Never coming back was the solution?"

"At the time, yes. Looking back it was one of the stupidest things I've ever done and I've regretted it every day since. I wanted to come back for you but I couldn't. Mama wouldn't let me," she tried explaining.

"You let your mother keep you away from a child you gave life to? I child you carried for 10 months?"

"You don't understand. After I had you I signed away my rights. I wasn't ready to be a mother. And once my signature was on those papers she told me if I left don't come back so I left and never looked back until I got word that she wasn't doing well."

"It was that easy, huh?" I asked hurt.

"Signing over your rights and just moving on in the world was easy huh? I was just a memory that you managed to push to the back of your mind."

"Satin, that is not true! I thought about you every single day. I carried your baby picture around with me everywhere. I've never forgotten about you."

"Answer me this, are there more?"

"Are there more what?"

"Kids. Did you have more?"

"Satin.." she started to say but I cut her off.

"DID. YOU. HAVE. MORE?" I asked her again loudly.

"Two. You have two siblings. A brother and a sister."

"Wow. Unbelievable. Instead of coming to get me you go off and have two more kids who were lucky enough to have you. Was I not good enough?"

"It's not like that Satin!"

"IT IS LIKE THAT! Instead of being a mother to me you go and have two more to replace me. That's why you were able to act like I didn't exist all of these years."

"I'm here now dammit! That counts for something baby," she tried to argue back as she tried touching my face but I backed away from her.

"Leave. Go. Leave!!!"

"Satin."

"I said leave!" I yelled. I was hurt and I had every reason to feel that way.

Instead of saying anything else she backed away from before turning around to walk to the front door. Making it to the front door she stopped for a brief moment before turning around and taking a look back at me and I quickly looked away. I didn't want her to see the tears that had fallen from my eyes. I didn't want or need her to know just how damaged she caused me to be. Finally, I released a sigh as I heard the door close.

A relationship with my mother wasn't an option at the moment. I just wasn't ready to let that door open. I wasn't open to allowing her into my world. She didn't deserve to. She didn't deserve me.

Dream

"Dreamy?" I heard Mega call out to me as I started waking up out of my sleep.

"Hmm?" I responded back as I snuggled closer to him. Every since the party we've been up under each other. I literally went to work and brought my ass home to make sure that I was here to greet him whenever he got back from doing whatever it was he be out doing.

Things were good between the two of us at the moment and I wanted them to stay that way. I even fell back from talking with Sosa. Things with her and I were weird. I was beginning to I guess develop a little crush on her. After the way, she licked my kitty I was starting to wonder what sex with her would be like had I allowed it to go any further than it did and to be honest that kinda freaked me out a bit. I wasn't gay. I liked men. I would someday probably marry a man so these little feelings or whatever you want to call them that I started to feel for her had to go.

I didn't see a future with her, at least not the way she did. She was cool as fuck to hang with and talk to but I couldn't let things go further than that. I have to make a mental noteto talk to her. She doesn't deserve to be led on and Mega doesn't deserve to be lied to. I liked Mega. I cared about him a lot and as much shit as I talk there was something different about him. Something that I couldn't and wouldn't let go of.

"You wouldn't lie to me, right?" he asked me in my ear.

"Huh?"

"You heard me. You wouldn't lie to me, right?"

"No, why?"

"So who's Sosa?"

Fuck! How did he know about her? Isn't ironic how I just said I had to end things between Sosa and I and he goes and ask about the bitch? I really wasn't trying to have this conversation with him. I wanted to just dead things with her first and just hope and pray that he never found out about her. Now, look. Fuck my life.

Swallowing the lump that had formed in my throat, I took a deep breath before responding. "A friend," I told him and I felt him separate himself from me.

"A friend? What kind of friend Dream?"

"She's uh, she's a friend. What's up with all the questions?"

"Dream!"

"Mega!"

"Shorty, until you can be honest with me we ain't got shit to talk about," he told me as he tried to get out of bed but I began pulling on his arm. This was it. This was my only chance, to be honest about the situation but I couldn't. He would look at me funny and I didn't want that. I didn't want him judging me. I didn't want anyone judging me.

"Where you going? I told you she's a friend."

"And you're lying. Look you need to get your shit together. I'm out here breaking laws and shit while you out here bumpin' pussies with some bitch that wants to be a man and not once did you think to tell me about it."

"Nigga I ain't ever bump a pussy in my muthafuckin' life. Don't do me! I told you she's just a fucking friend!" I yelled loudly as he shook my hand off him. I had yelled so loud I wasn't sure who I was trying to convince more. Him or myself.

"Dream, baby girl these messages say otherwise. When you're ready to be truthful hit me up until then don't call me. I only asked for you to be patient with a nigga. That's it."

"And I am tellin' you the truth. She's just a friend Mega!"

"You heard what I said," he told me as he gathered his things to go.

"So that's it? You just gonna leave? Fuck what I'm saying about her being a friend? Really?"

"Dream I'm not 'bout to play wit your ass. You cute ma but I ain't no sucka ass nigga. When you get ya mind right hit me."

"Fine. Have it your way," I told him and he chuckled before walking out and leaving me sitting in the bed alone. I couldn't even be mad at him. I was mad at my damn self for being so fuckin' stupid.

****

One week later

"Can I get another Apple Martini?" I asked the bartender as I sat at the bar waiting on Isabella.

It has been an entire week since Mega has walked out on me and I was miserable as ever. I hadn't even been out except for work and even then I didn't want to be out. I just didn't want to do life. He really had me in my feelings and this weak shit has never been me but I was ready to just say fuck it and give in since he was sticking to his word.

"Hey baby love," Isabella greeted me as she kissed my cheek.

"What's the problem?" she asked as she saw the bartender place my Martini in front of me.

"Must be serious if you're drinking a damn Martini. What happened?"

"Mega left me."

"What? Why? What happened?"

"The dyke bitch."

"He found out? How?"

"Some messages."

"Dream, I can't see him leaving you over some harmless messages. They were harmless, right?" she questioned and I didn't answer, I just took a sip from my glass.

"Dream! What you do? Send her some pictures or something?" still I said nothing and she started laughing at me.

"Bitch you sent your pussy through the phone?"

"It's not funny Izzyyyyy," I whined as I poked my lip out.

"It is funny. Satin told your hot pussy ass you were playing with fire and look, she was right. You can't be mad at anyone but yourself Dream. You made this mess and now you have to clean it up."

"He thinks I fucked her or as he said bumped pussies with her. I'm not gay Iz!"

"Well did you?"

"Bitch no," I responded back lying like hell as I sucked my teeth. Well technically it wasn't a lie. I didn't bump or rub pussies with her nor did I pleasure her. She just ate my pussy and I hauled ass out of there.

"I'm actually offended that you thought that I would even do some shit like bump pussies."

"I don't know Dream. You never crossed me as the type to entertain another woman but yet you did so I can't be too sure boo. It's all love though."

"How do I fix it, Izzy? How do I make him believe that I didn't do what he's accusing me of?"

"First you need to cut her off. I'm talking completely. Do not keep her as a friend. Secondly, you force him to see you. He'll have no reason not to listen to you if you bombard him."

"I haven't spoken to her since. She just keeps texting me and I keep ignoring her. I thought she'd get the picture but it ain't working."

"Block her. Why you acting stupid?"

"Bitch!"

"I'm just saying. You know what you need to do so do it. Sitting here at this bar ain't gonna fix it. You have to. So either you boss the hell up or you can let somebody else take him off your hands. The choice is yours."

"I knew there was a reason I called you and not Satin. You've always been the logical one. You know? The one with common sense," I said with a giggle and a burp accidentally slipped out.

"Oops!"

"Okay grown ass man that was nasty and so not ladylike. And as far as Satin goes, you didn't call her because you didn't want to hear the I told you so speech and you knew I wasn't going to give it to you. You're grown at the end of the day and you know right from wrong. You also know that everything has consequences. You know all of this but you still wanted to be curious and now your feelings are hurt because he don't want to talk to you. Serves your ass right."

"Whatever. Anyways enough about me. What's up with you?"

"Nothing. Sincere and I are good," she said through a forced smile.

"You sure?"

"Yeah. You know he wants a baby but I don't think I can give him that so every time he brings up children I change the subject."

"Why don't you think you can give him a baby? Y'all haven't even been trying."

"That's the thing, I think he has though. I can't find my birth control pills. You know I don't want any kids. At least not now. I honestly think he hid them bitches from me," she said with a serious face and I couldn't help but laugh.

"Isabella, do you hear yourself right now. Who hides birth control pills?" I asked as I continued to laugh.

"It's not funny. I can't find them. I keep them in the same spot and now I can't find them. They've been missing for about a month now."

"You work at a hospital. Why not get another one prescribed or write your own prescription?"

"I'm not going to jail behind no damn birth control stupid."

"Well, ma'am I don't know what you want me to say."

"I swear you're no help," she fussed as she grabbed her purse.

"Drunk ass hoe."

"You're marrying him, Izzy. Give him a baby. Marriage is about compromising. If you ain't tryna compromise, why marry him?"

"Because I love him."

"If you love him then give him a baby. It's not that hard Isabella. What are you afraid of? You have the fairytale love. The fiancé, the great job, college degree. You have it all. You have the perfect life. Meanwhile, Joi is mourning her marriage, Satin is in denial about her feelings, Kori is smashing Joi's husbands and me, I'm just all fucked up. You have what we want."

"I just, I just don't know about babies."

"Well, my friend I don't know what to tell you," I told her as I finished my drink.

"Seems to me you have some thinking to do. I'm going home. Let's go."

"Dream I am not letting you drive like this, I'll bring you home."

"Whatever as long as I get there."

After paying for my tab, Isabella and I got in her car and like the good friend that she is she brought me home. The whole time she was driving I couldn't help but think about Mega. It was time that I started to be honest with myself. I wanted him. I wanted him and only him and I had to get him back even if that meant being the bigger person.

I was going, to be honest, and I was also going to apologize. I felt like it was only right. If I was going to give Mega and I a fair chance I had to make some changes. I was gonna do exactly what Isabella suggested. I was about to boss the fuck up and go get my man. Well, I had to find him first but you get what I'm saying.

Isabella

I love Dream. I really do but she was really acting slow. I don't know why she thought she could just hide that Sosa girl from Mega. Our city is little as hell and I know he may not be from here but clearly, her shit got super sloppy. But who am I to judge? I believed my man was hiding my birth control pills from me so I don't even have room to talk about anyone else's relationship. I will say though I knew it would be a matter of time before she got caught up. What's done in the dark will always come to the light eventually.

Speaking about that I truly did believe that Sincere was hiding my birth control pills. I've never been irresponsible when it came down to things especially my birth control. For all I know I could be pregnant right now. Oh shit, can I be pregnant? I have been gaining a little weight lately but I was chopping that up to happy engagement weight. Our relationship was flourishing. I mean other than the fact that he may have hid my pills from me everything was good.

"Iz..," Dream slurred taking me out of my thoughts as I drove her home.

"Wassup boo?"

"I.. I think.. I think I love him."

"Who?"

"Who else silly girl? Megaaa," she sung and I couldn't help but laugh.

"A blind man can see that baby," I replied back to her as I looked at her through the corner of my right eye.

"I'm just scared, you know? What if he gets bored with me? What if he meets someone prettier than me? Better than me?"

"He won't. I saw the way he looked at you and he adores you. Honestly, he does. He looked at you with so much lust and admiration. He looks at you the way Sin looks at me. He lights up. That man ain't thinking about nobody else but his Dreamy."

"I don't know. I just don't want to give my all to someone just to end up hurt again."

"You won't know unless you try," I told her and she just looked out the window.

I understand the fear of giving someone every part of you and not knowing the unknown. I get it. But I also know that you'll never know the outcome unless you try. These girls think Sincere and I have always had the perfect relationship and that couldn't be the furthest thing from the truth. We had our trying times but we worked through them. People don't see the work we put into making this thing work they just look at our relationship and see what we have.

Granted Sin never cheated on me or even disrespected me for that matter but I haven't always been the easiest to deal with. Yes, I knew when I first saw him, I wanted forever with him. However, I also didn't want to lose myself in the process of building that. I didn't want to lose my identity and in some way I still kind of feel like that. I don't mind becoming his wife as long as I can still maintain my independence and the moment we have children I believe I'll probably lose that and I don't want to. I'll be labeled as Isabella, Sincere's loving wife and mother to his children and not Isabella the loving, beautifully spirit individual.

And my career. That's another one of my concerns I have regarding children. I worked my ass off putting myself through school to become a Registered Nurse and I'm finally getting settled into a job in my field. Becoming pregnant can and will halt my life. Maybe I'm being selfish but what about me? Now that I think about it maybe this marriage idea isn't so great after all. Maybe we need to thoroughly think things through before we take that step.

Finally pulling up to Dream's apartment, I reached over and tapped her on her shoulder letting her know we made it. She was really drunk off her ass and there was no way in hell I was going to let her walk inside alone. Ain't no tellin who out here lurking and could possibly take advantage of her. That type of thing was not happening on my watch. If I had to, I'd even stay the night over her place. I'd just call Sin and let him know what's up and I can probably give his and my situation more thought.

Getting out of the car and walking around to the passenger side car door, I opened it up before grabbing her purse and helping her out. The whole time we were making our way to her apartment she just kept chanting Mega's name and I felt bad for her. As long as I've known Dream she's been what you would call a man-eater. Wasn't no settling down for her. I don't really know what she was like before she met us all but since Satin introduced her she's been just living her life as a single girl and I admired and respected that.

I never passed judgment because that's the beauty of everyone being their own person. No one person is the same, especially within our circle. Every last one of us were different and viewed relationships differently. My only thing with Dream right now, is her putting up this facade like she didn't care about this man . She kinda played herself if you ask me.

"Dream, your keys?" I asked her once we made it to the door.

"My purse. I think," she responded drunkenly.

"I gotta peeeee Izzy."

"Oh gosh, Dream your drunk ass better not piss on my feet," I whined as I finally found her keys. Unlocking the door and letting ourselves in Dream immediately took off and headed in the direction of the bathroom as I locked up. Taking my phone out of my pocket I glanced at the time and decided to just call my baby so he wouldn't be worried.

"Wassup sweetheart? Where you at? It's late," he asked back to back and I just gave him a light giggle before responding.

"I'm at Dream's. She got drunk so I drove her home. I think Ima stay here tonight just to make sure she's good. I can't leave her like this."

"Damn she got that drunk? I thought I was gonna be able to get some."

"Seriously Sin, my vag needs a break."

"A break? Yeah aight."

"Yes, a break. What if I end up with a prolapsed uterus or something?"

"A what? The hell is that?"

"When your uterus falls out of your vagina and I'll have to keep popping it back up there."

"What the fuck? Isabella my dick just went limp. Go take care of ya girl," he said grossed out causing me to laugh.

"Oh, now you want to hang up ? Soft ass. See you tomorrow bae. I love you."

"Yeah aight. Love you too."

"No good night or nothing?"

"Good night Iz. Is that better?"

"Yupp! Good night!" I told him quickly as I hung up the phone and placing it on one of her end tables.

"Dream? Dreammm?" I tried calling out to her but she didn't respond.

Walking throughout her apartment I found her on top of her bed with her ass out as she snored loudly. *Damn shame.* I giggled to myself as I shook my head. Looking around for something to cover her up with I noticed she had a group photo of us all at my graduation sitting on her dresser and that made me smile. We were all smiling so wide. There was so much love in that photo you could literally feel it.

"Ahh good times," I said to myself.

"I'm going to miss that bitch," Dream said out of nowhere and I turned around and saw her sitting up in bed with her curls all over her head.

"I thought you were asleep."

"I was but I heard your movements. I can't sleep with people walking around me."

"My bad. I'm sorry."

"It's cool. What you still doing here anyways?"

"I'm gonna stay with you tonight."

"I don't need a babysitter. I'm grown," she said getting underneath her blanket.

"But if you're staying I need for you to lay down."

"Don't touch me Dream. You know your ass is straddling the fence."

"First off watch your mouth. I don't want you and if I did you know you'd let me rub ya titties."

"You're so nasty," I giggled as I got into the bed with her.

"But you still got into the bed with me. Good night Iz," she told me and turned over so that her back was facing me.

"Good night meanie," I said back at her before quickly saying a prayer to myself and closing my eyes.

Joi

I couldn't wait until I was able to walk around without this damn air cast. It was starting to be a pain in my ass. One of my hips were higher than the other and it's causing my back to hurt which means I don't even want to go anywhere. I rather just sit at home and have my leg propped up but being in this house alone was beginning to be depressing. I was finding myself drowning in emotions and I kept reliving Kori and Jacob being in bed together. I'm still disgusted by it all.

I kept telling the girls I was cool but I wasn't. I was mad as hell and I wanted answers. I wanted to know why. I wanted to know why did Kori do what she did. I wanted to know why Jacob couldn't keep his dick in his pants. For the life of me, I couldn't wrap my head around this shit. Hearing knocks at my front door I got up and limped my way to the door opening it for my guest. Jacob. I know you're probably calling me all types of stupid but it ain't even that type of party. I said I wanted answers and I was going to get them. The sooner I got closure, the sooner I could move on.

"Wassup?" he asked me as I walked back to the sofa where I was originally sitting as fast as this cast would allow me to. Finally making it back I sat down just as he sat on my ottoman.

"Why? Why her?" I asked looking into his eyes but he looked away. Probably embarrassed because technically the her I was referring to was born a man.

"Shit, Joi. I don't. I don't know. It just happened. I don't want to talk about that."

"It ain't about what you want to talk about. I didn't call you over here for a social call. You owe me the damn truth!"

"It just happened. We ran into each other one night and we been fucking since. Well were. I didn't know she was. Man you know what the fuck I'm tryna say."

"What that she was a man. That she's the same fucking Kori that we went to high school with. You know the same Kori that was my gay best friend? You see what happens when you can't keep your skinny dick in your pants?" I smirked at him.

"Fuck is you talkin' bout?" he asked angrily as his top lip curled up. He was mad. He was questioning his manhood. It was all in his eyes. I saw right through him.

"Boy pussy must've been feeling good if you got sloppy with your cheating. I'm not even hurt. I'm mad at this point. Mad that the two people I trusted the most could just betray me the way that y'all did. I'm even more so disgusted with you because it was bitch after bitch. Was I not enough? Hmm? Was I not good to you? I gave you EVERYTHING! EVERY FUCKING THING I HAD YET I WASN'T ENOUGH. WE WEREN'T ENOUGH!" I yelled as tears involuntarily fell from my eyes. I told myself I wasn't going to cry. I told myself he wouldn't have that satisfaction of seeing me so broken.

"Joi," he called out reaching for me but I swatted his hand away.

"I HATE YOU!"

"I'm sorry baby. I swear I'm so fucking sorry. You gotta believe me. I never meant to hurt you."

"JUST STOP! STOP LYING! YOU'RE NOT SORRY! YOU'RE SORRY YOU GOT CAUGHT. YOU WILL NOT HAVE AN OPPORTUNITY TO HURT ME AGIAN!"

"We can work this out. We've been together this long why just throw it all away?" he asked me and I almost slapped the shit out of him. Did he really just have the balls to say that? I was so baffled I just looked at him in awe.

"Excuse me? You're playing, right? Work it out? Ain't shit to fucking work out. You ended us the moment you stuck your dick into the first bitch. I was just so hung up on having a husband I turned a blind eye but not anymore. I meant what I said. You will never have the opportunity to hurt me again."

"So that's it huh? You just think you gonna leave me?"

"I don't think anything, I *know* that I'm leaving you," I stated matter of factly and before I could move he had grabbed me by my throat with his right hand as his left hand roamed my body causing me to become paralyzed in fear.

"This belongs to me, you hear me?" he said into my ear as he licked the side of my face causing my skin to crawl.

Taking both of my hands I clawed at his face trying my hardest to get him off of me but he wouldn't let up it just angered him and his left hand that was once roaming my body had went across my face. *SLAP!* I was so stunned because I never saw this side of him. I didn't know this Jacob. The man on top of me resembled Satan himself. Even though my face was still stinging I still tried to fight back but I was no match for him.

He was smiling at me in a sadistic way as he continued to assault me and I knew then he was enjoying this. He wanted control and in some fucked up way he had gotten that. The more I fought the more restless I became. I had no desire or energy to keep fighting him off of me and once I heard him unzip his zipper to his Levi jeans I forced myself to space out. He was gonna rape me. I wouldn't give him what he wanted so instead he was going to take it.

Drifting off to a happy place I became numb to what was going on. Still not letting go of my neck he shoved his dick into my dry walls. He just humped and pumped on top of me as I stared off into space allowing him to do whatever he wanted to do to my body. It didn't matter that I wasn't moving or even moaning he still had sex with me as if it was consensual. As if I was enjoying it.

After about three minutes he began thrusting harder and faster and I knew the end was near and I couldn't wait. Jacob had violated me in the worst way imaginable and I felt disgusted. I felt weak. I felt like less of a woman. I felt like some random whore off the street versus his wife.

"Grrrrrrr ughhhhh," he grunted spilling all of his demon seeds inside of me. Getting from up off of me and walking away and I just layed there. I layed in the same spot as his cum seeped out of my opening feeling worthless.

Crying silently to myself as tears cascaded down the sides of my face I watched him out of the corner of my eye as he grabbed his things to go. The moment he walked in my direction I closed my eyes tight hoping and praying that death came to me but it didn't. He bent down and kissed my lips before walking away again and walking out of my house.

As soon as I heard the door close I found some strength and crawled to the front door and locked it. I couldn't believe the man I loved turned out to be a monster. He had turned into somebody I didn't recognize and that night I cried. I cried for myself. I cried for the woman I had become. The moment he slid inside of my essence without permission I knew I'd never be the same. My life as I knew it had changed.

How did I end up here?

Satin

"Satin how's Kori?" my grandmother asked me as I brushed her hair in a ponytail. After the argument, I had with my mother I needed to be around my nana. She was my safetynet and with everything around me going to shit I just needed a little bit of her sunshine.

"Haven't spoken to her," I replied back keeping it short.

"And why is that? It's not like y'all to go this long without speaking to one another."

"You know how Kori is."

"Yeah and I also know how you are. What's going on Satin?"

"Nothing. Nothing you need to worry your pretty little head about," I told her right before kissing her cheek.

"Grams, guess what?!"

"What? You finally found a man?" she joked.

"Ha ha ha. Very funny. But no, I signed up for hair school. I'm gonna make you proud. Own that salon I've always spoke about."

"I'm already proud of you baby. Grandma is always proud of you. You hear me?"

"I hear you nana."

"Now all we gotta do is get you a man so you can have some babies."

"GRANDMA!" I yelled as I laughed.

"What chile? If I never caught you going down on that Manish ass boy that time I would've thought you were into the licky licky," she said as she side eyed me.

"The licky licky?"

"Yeah, girl. You know what I'm talking about. I'm old but I ain't crazy."

"You know what? That's enough for today. I think I'm gonna get ready to go," I giggled and she playfully hit my arm.

"You better sit your hot ass right there. We ain't done talking crazy girl."

"Grandma you just don't want me to leave. It's okay to admit that. I know you miss me. I miss you too."

"Of course, I miss my baby and since we're on the subject of missing people, Satin your mother -," she started to say but I cut her off. I didn't come to talk about her.

"No disrespect grandma but I don't really want to talk about her right now."

"Satin, she's your mother."

"She's an egg donor. I'm gonna get ready to go," I mentioned with a sigh. I don't understand why she kept pushing the issue. I wanted nothing to do with that lady and I needed for my grandmother to respect my wishes.

****

"Come with me to Miami," Dream said to me with a serious look on her face as she sat across from me at her kitchen table smoking a cigarette.

"Bitch what?"

"Come to Miami with me."

"Dream.."

"Satin, I'm going either way but I want you to come with me. I need you to come with me."

"What's in Miami Dream and how are we paying for this?" I asked her as I shuffled the deck of cards I had in my hands.

"Money obviously but Mega. Satin he left me. And I know he's in Miami. I feel it. You coming with me or what bitch? Stop asking questions."

"What happened with you and Mega? The fuck did you do Dream?"

"Tell me you're coming with me first and I'll tell you."

"Fuck it. I might regret this later but Ima go," I told her just as a knock was at her door.

"That's why you my bitch," she said as she got up to answer the door. "What are you doing here?" I heard her ask whoever it was at the door and you know me being me I had to get up and be nosey.

As I tiptoed quietly I saw that it was the dyke hoe. See Dream had some explaining to do. There's nothing she could possibly say at this point to convince me that she wasn't feeling this girl. If there wasn't nothing going on with them then why was she still around? Bringing my attention back to what was taking place in front of me I continued to eavesdrop.

"Why you avoiding me Dream?" Sosa asked her.

"I'm not. I've been busy," Dream responded back to her in a hush tone.

"That seems to be your excuse a lot lately. What's really going on?"

"Nothing. I just, I've been thinking. Maybe we should just chill out."

"Chill out huh? Why?"

"I'm not gay Sosa."

"And I'm aware of that."

"Are you really? Because I feel like you just keep trying to force me into believing that I am. Forcing me into believing that there's something between us."

"Nah, baby girl that's all you. You feel some sort of way because you don't know what to do with what you're feeling and I mean it's cool but you need to be real with yourself. I ain't gon' beg your ass to fuck with me though so Ima let you go and do you. You take care, aight?" Sosa told her.

"We can still be friends, right? I mean it doesn't have to be this way," Dream pleaded to her shocking the hell out of me.

"Nah. We can't. I can't be friends with someone I'm interested in. Shit wasn't supposed to even go down like that but it did and now you want me to be cool with just being your friend? Nah ma I can't do that" she said and turned to walk away.

"Sosa! Sosa!"

"You like her," I said startling Dream as she stood in her doorway.

"Not now Satin."

"No Dream how about now. Obviously, you've been over here keeping secrets."

"For once Satin, shut up please," Dream said to me irritated as she closed the door and walked back into the kitchen.

"Now I gotta shut up. Ain't this some shit. Is she the reason he left?" I asked her but she didn't say anything. She didn't have to because the moment she looked me in my eyes I knew it was true.

"Aw shit Dream. How'd you let this happen?"

"I don't know. I got lonely. He was out of town and I started spending time with her. Talking to her. I didn't think I'd catch feelings. I'm not gay Satin. She was different."

"I'm not judging. Trust me. But who do you want more?"

"Huh?"

"You heard me. Who is it that you want more?"

"You know I care about Mega more. That was just a dumb ass question."

"Was it really? Because it seems like to me you care about her just as much. I don't know how you got yourself into this mess but you need to figure it out before you go jumping on planes and finding Mega. Be sure that he's who you want. I'm with whichever you choose."

"Look I care about Sosa but I'm not into women. Mega is for me. Him leaving made me realize that. If it comes down to choosing I'll choose him. Sosa was a great confidant but I can't live without Mega. I don't want to friend," she stated as her eyes began to water and I hugged her.

Dream is so hard all of the time so seeing her in such a vulnerable state spoke volumes. This was real. She meant what she said and if going to Miami to get her man is what she wanted to do then I was going with her. Fuck it.

Kori

It's been a few weeks since it came out that I was having an affair with Jacob and I still hadn't heard from him. He blocked me on everything and I had no way of contacting him and I was beginning to grow tired. I wanted a life with him and if he allowed himself to be open he would want a life with me as well. Call me crazy but I honestly did believe that.

"Kori you need to get out of this house. Hiding ain't gon' fix anything," Destiny said to me as she walked into the spare bedroom I was now occupying at her house.

"I'm not hiding!"

"Then what you call it?"

"I just need some time," I whined.

"Time for what? Kori, you created this mess and now you have to deal with it and fix it. If you was so worried about the repercussions then maybe you should've thought twice before lying to everybody."

"You judging me?"

"Yes, I am actually. You was wrong as hell in all aspects. You not only betrayed your friend, you lied to him as well. How you ain't tell the nigga you had a dick?"

"First of all, you shouldn't be judging me when you ain't no better. You've messed with a few married men so don't go there. Now, as far as everything else goes he should've been mine. I've been in love with him my whole life. She knew that!"

"The difference between you and I is the fact that I ain't never sucked and fucked a nigga that had any dealings with people I claim to love but you dear, you did and it's fucked up. Let's not forget he didn't even know you were a dude. Most niggas would fucking kill you. Do you not understand how serious this shit is?" she asked as she looked at me with pity.

"Jacob ain't gonna do shit. He's not even built like that," I said confidently.

"Don't be too sure. Get your shit together Kori. I love you and you know this but I can't be involved in your mess. Word around town is that Jacob been asking about you. I don't need that type of mess near me."

"So what you saying?"

"I'm saying I love you but you gotta find you some other place to go. This shit is so wrong. You've been here for weeks Kor, just leave town and don't look back at least for now. Maybe wait until things die down to come back."

"I thought you had my back Des?"

"I do. But I can't be involved in this shit anymore. You said you needed a few days and that turned into weeks. I gotta head out to work. I love you. You know that, right?"

"Whatever bitch. You love me but you putting me out. Some friend you are."

"I do love you but Kori I don't need this shit. You know I'm going through a custody battle already tryna get my kids back. I'm finally on the right path of getting my shit together and I can't get distracted or involved in things that can potentially hurt that. Stop being selfish."

"NO, you stop being selfish! Don't worry I'll be gone by time you get home. Have a good day Destiny."

"You for real right now?" she asked me but I didn't answer I just mugged her. How could she just abandon me when I needed her? That was some real selfish ass shit if you asked me.

"Alright then Kori," she went on to say just before she sucked her teeth and walking out.

Getting up I started to get my things together so I could leave. I was going to take her advice and leave town. Maybe go down to Atlanta or head west to San Francisco. I wasn't sure. I just needed to make my way to the airport. I'll decide when I get there.

Looking around and making sure I grabbed everything I stood up and the hair on my back instantly stood up but I just shrugged it off thinking it was paranoia.

"Destiny, you still here?" I asked out loud but didn't get a response and that was a bit weird. Right before I turned around someone said something.

"Nah but I'm here," Jacob said as he closed the door and I froze.

"You embarrassed me. You lied to me. The whole time I thought you were a woman. That's some sick shit Kori," he said and I heard him walk closer to me but I couldn't move. It was something off in his voice that had me scared. He didn't sound with it.

"I'm s-s-s-sorry," I stuttered over my words.

"Sorry, huh? You think I'm a fucking faggot? YOU THINK I'M A FUCKING QUEER LIKE YOU?" he yelled at me and pushed me forward causing me to hit my head on the corner of the dresser. "STAND UP PUSSY!"

"Jacob, we can talk about this. You don't have to do this," I said as I cried.

"AIN'T. SHIT. TO. TALK. ABOUT! YOU GOT THESE NIGGAS LAUGHING AT ME LIKE I'M SOME GAY ASS MUTHAFUCKA," he yelled again just as he kicked me in my back making me fall completely on my face. Turning me over so that I was looking at him and punched me in the face hitting me in the nose making it break instantly as blood dripped from it. Repeatedly he punched me in the face until I couldn't take it anymore and mustered up the courage and kicked him in his dick causing him to stumble back.

"Ughhhh," I groaned as I tried picking myself up off of the floor. I needed to get the fuck up outtahere. Grabbing the closest thing to me which was a trophy and the moment he charged at me I hit him in the head with it. I was beginning to feel a little light-headed from losing so much blood.

Making a run for it I grabbed my bag and began staggering to the door but was stopped when I heard a gun cock back and I felt a bullet enter my back causing me to fall to my knees and another shot through my skull. This was it. Destiny was right. I made this mess and now I was paying for it with my life.

"I'm sorry," I whispered as I fell face first on the floor. If God saw me through this, this would be a miracle but I didn't deserve that. I did wrong by everyone and I was paying for that. Closing my eyes my breathing became shallow and blood continued to pour out of me.

I never meant to hurt anyone, I just was trying to live my life. Live my happiness.

Hassan

Last night took a L but tonight I bounce back. Wake up every

morning by the night I count stacks. Knew that ass was real when

I hit, it bounce back. Last night took a L but tonight I bounce back.

Boy, I been broke as hell, cashed a check and bounced back. D- town

LAX every week I bounce back. If you a real one, then you know how

to bounce back.

I was sitting in my office of my jewelry store counting up this money as I listened to this Big Sean track play. I had fallen off a lil bit after that shit with Satin but a nigga head was back in the game. I fucked with her the long way but if she wasn't tryna hear me out I wasn't gonna force her ass to. I meant what I said when I popped up at her crib. If she wanted me out I was gonna respect her wishes. Chasing bitches ain't ever been my thing anyway.

Don't get me wrong Satin was everything I needed and then some. I'm talkin' the full fucking package. She was beautiful, sweet, kind, funny, nasty and last but not least a good fucking person. She had me feeling like I could drop all the women I was currently entertaining just for her including Halima and I've been rockin' with her the longest. That's how much I was feeling her but she ain't even give ya boy a chance.

Speaking on Halima I was sensing that she wasn't into our relationship as much as she used to be but then again I could be playing a part in that cause I wasn't into it either. I fucked with her out of loyalty and because when I approached her on this shit she was cool with it but now that we're older maybe this type of thing wasn't for her. Business was on the up and up between the two of us but personal wise things we're just weird.

Knock! Knock! I heard causing me to look up. Yelling for whoever it was to come in, I glanced up to see that it was the devil herself. Halima.

"Hey handsome," she greeted me as she took a seat in front of my desk.

"Wassup gorgeous?" I asked her back as I placed some money in a duffle bag to take to the bank.

"We need to talk."

"What's on your mind?"

"I've been thinking about relocating. For good."

"I'm all ears," I told her as I sat back and observed her body language. She was nervous. She kept playing with her nails and she couldn't look at me. She's never been nervous around me in the ten plus years that we've known each other.

"I want to move to New York for good. I miss my family," she expressed before pausing to look at me.

"What's stopping you? You can still run the club from up there. You have a great management team."

"You. I don't think we can be in this relationship with the two of us living in separate cities."

"Word?"

"Yeah but that's not it. I don't want the club anymore. I don't want the responsibility of it. I want to sell it."

"You've got to be shittin' me Halima."

"Just hear me out bae. I can open up a beauty bar in Harlem and later down the line if I'm missing the action of the adult entertainment world I can just open a new one. I know I could make a killin' up north."

"You can't just sell the club without me and I'm not selling it."

"You serious right now? Why can't I sell MY club, Hassan? It's mine! I just put you on to it!" she said raising her voice.

"The club brings in a lot of profit I can't let you sell it. If you want to get rid of your portion I can buy it from you or bring in someone who may be interested in it," I reasoned with her.

"But-" she started to say but I held my hand up letting her know there was no negotiating.

"Whatever, do whatever you want Hassan. Arguing with you is pointless. I leave in three weeks. Get to work," she told me as she stood up and ironed out the fake wrinkles in the body-hugging dress she was wearing.

"Halima, how much you asking for?" I asked her as I tugged on my beard.

"175k. I'm not taking anything less."

"Kinda pricey don't you think? For fifty percent?"

"I know that isn't Hassan complaining about money."

"Never that, stop clowning."

"I want my money, you got it!" she winked just as she prepared to walk out of my office bumpin into Mega on her way out.

"Hey Mega, I ain't know you were in town."

"Wassup pretty lady? I just landed not too long ago."

"Well, I hope you enjoy yourself while you're out here. Stay outta trouble!" she went on to say before making her exit as Mega walked in taking a seat right where Halima had.

"What's good bro?" I asked him as he ran his hands over his face before rubbing his right hand over his head. He looked stressed.

"Ain't shit. Needed to get away for a lil bit. You know how that goes"

"How's business?"

"Shit good. Had a little situation I had to take care of but shit smooth, feel me?"

"Cool," I told him before sitting up.

"Got a proposal for you."

"What's that?"

"You still tryna clean up your money? Go legit and shit?"

"Hell muthafuckin' yeah. I can't be pushing weight my whole life. Nigga I'm almost 40 fuckin' years old. Fuck you think?"

"Halima selling her portion of the club. You want in?"

"How much?"

"175K but that's small shit."

"Count me in nigga. Draw up the paperwork."

"You sure?"

"Positive. I'm with it," he said just as his phone rang and he silenced the call and that stressed out look was back on his face.

"You sure you aight?" I asked him before I lit a Cuban Cigar, offering him one but he declined.

"I'm straight. That's Dream's hoe ass."

"Whoa whoa whoa. The fuck I miss? You disrespectin the lil lady now?"

"Shorty been playing me. Got me feeling like some sucka or some shit."

"Satin's friend, right?"

"Yeah. She been fuckin with some dyke ass bitch."

"You lying," I told him as I started laughing but he sat there with a straight face just as his phone rang again.

"Nigga, you lost ya girl to a bitch with a plastic dick? That's wicked"

"Bruh I had the half of mind to fuck her up but I didn't. I just left. I ain't even gonna lie though, that shit was embarrassing. You know how fucked up shit gotta be to lose ya girl to another girl? Not no regular girl either, a dyke. Shit is crazy my nigga," he stressed.

"You really care about her?"

"Of course nigga!"

"Hear her out then," I told him but he just fanned his hand at me in a dismissive manner.

I was serious. If he cared about ol' girl the way I think he does then he needs to talk to her. Walking away from her isn't solving shit. I've seen brodie with a bunch of broads but he never looked at any of them hoes the way he looked at her so I knew it was real when he brought her down here. He had something good and he knew it. He was just being stubborn just like Satin's ass.

I ain't no cupid or no shit like that but finding something real was rare and Mega needed to put his pride aside and just hear her out. Maybe then his girl can convince Satin to do the same because I was missing my lil baby somethin' serious.

Dream

"Y'all bitches really leaving?" Isabella asked us as we got into her car. I didn't respond. I just kept calling Mega. I needed him to answer. I was gonna feel stupid as fuck if I went all the way down to Miami and his ass wasn't even there.

"Dream wants to go so I'm tagging along. I'm just here for support," Satin replied and Isabella laughed.

"For y'all sake I hope his ass is down there."

"I don't think this is a good idea," I said out loud and they both stopped and looked at me.

"DREAM!" Satin yelled and I rolled my eyes.

"I know you ain't do all this just to chicken out. Bitch don't play with me."

"Satin!" Isabella said as she giggled.

"Relax. What's wrong Dream? I can turn around if you want."

"Izzy you really fallin into her mess? She don't know what she talkin' bout. Drive this damn car."

"I, I just don't know anymore. I was so sure but now that the time has come I just think maybe we shouldn't go. What if he's with another bitch? Or what if he's not even down there?"

"Look," Satin said with a sigh.

"We have one or two options. We can stay here and give it some more time and hopefully he comes to his senses or I can take one for the team and reach out to Hassan when we make it down there. I ain't fuckin' with the nigga but if anyone knows where Mega is it'll be him. He's our only connection to him."

"She's right. But trust me Dream something is tellin' me you're doing the right thing," Isabella chimed in.

"Y'all.. I don't know."

"Fuck it, I'm calling Hassan's ugly ass"

"Now you know that man ain't ugly. Hell if I wasn't engaged to Sincere I'd probably give him some."

"Don't push your luck you lil light skinned heffa."

"Thought you didn't care about him."

"You know I be lying," Satin said as she laughed.

"Now lemme see your phone, wait nevermind, you might try callin' him and Ima have to fight you. Dream let me see your phone."

"Satin!"

"Ain't no Satin bihhhh. Nah for real though. You tryna go find your man or what?"

"What if he doesn't want to be with me anymore?" I asked looking out of the window.

"I can't handle rejection. I'm not built for that."

"Girl boo. That man wants you. I keep tellin' you that I know what I saw. He cares about you. He's just mad. Your job is to make him unmad."

I was hearing everything Satin and Izzy was saying but it wasn't as easy as they were making it seem. Mega wasn't mad about Sosa, he was mad that I lied. I lied straight to his face when he knew the truth. I think I even saw a little disappointment in his eyes when he looked at me and I hated that. I wasn't setting out to hurt him, I was just lonely and he wasn't there. I wanted to feel wanted and Sosa wanted me. She filled a void that was there.

****

"You good boo?" Satin asked me as we sat at Wet Willies in South Beach enjoying a couple of drinks and wings.

"I'm alright. He's still not answering any of my phone calls though. I'm just ready to give up. I'm not gonna beg him to talk to me." I told her as I took a sip from my drink.

"Can I ask you something?"

"What Satin?"

"Why weren't you just honest when he asked you from the beginning? Maybe you wouldn't even be going through this."

"What you mean? I told him she was just my friend."

"Which was a lie Dream. You were starting to like that girl."

"Satin!"

"Dream, seriously. We're friends, right?" she asked me and I nodded my head yes.

"So why not at least tell me what was going on with you and ol' girl? I knew it was more when you started hanging out with her more often than usual. You fuck her?" she asked and I damn near choked on my drink before finally responding.

"No, I ain't fuck her."

"Hoe you did something. I know you."

"I didn't do anything. We just made out a couple of times and maybe I let her finger me once or twice and eat me out but that's it. Nothing else happened."

"Y'all childish as hell. Who still getting finger fucked in their late twenties?"

"Why you always got something to say?"

"Wouldn't be me if I didn't have anything to say. But seriously though, you should've listened to me when I told you to leave her ass alone when she approached you but noooo you had to act like a kid and do the complete opposite."

"You know? I kinda liked your ass better when you were getting some dick. Your attitude has been funky as hell since you cut Hassan's lil cute ass off."

"You definitely just tried it. Besides Hassan is the least of my worries."

"That's what your mouth says but I'm sure your vagina says otherwise. How you cut off consistent dick?"

"I know you ain't talking Ms. Ima try some pussy out to see if I like it. The fuckin' nerveeee," she teased and I couldn't help but laugh at her crazy ass.

"I told you I didn't have sex with her. She did have some soft lips though, I'm kinda sad I ain't take advantage of them," I responded back to her with my lip poked out.

"Look at you, just nasty! That's enough alcohol for you, Ms. Thang."

"I ain't even do anything."

"I don't know Dream. Now that you crushing on these hoes I can't trust you to remain a child of God around anyone anymore with your sexually freed ass."

"Satin you never pegged me to be a hater but right now you are showing signs of one."

"Never a hater boo," she told me as she blew me a kiss.

"Yeah, aight. You ready? This drink done made me tired," I told her as I got a notification on my phone letting me know I had a text message and I saw that it was from Mega.

Mega: Wassup

Me: Oh now you know me.

Mega: You been blowing me up. Wassup?

Me: So you seen me calling yet you ain't answer?

Mega: You know why.

Me: Whatever. Where are you?

Mega: I'm not in town right now.

Me: Okay.. So where are you? With your new girlfriend?

Mega: Cut your shit Dreamy. I'm not thinkin' about these bitches

Me: Still not answering my question.

Mega: Miami.

I wasn't even gonna let him know I was out here. I'd just hit him up tomorrow. At least he wasn't ignoring me anymore. Grabbing our things Satin and I walked out hand in hand and for the first time in the past few weeks was finally wearing a smile. Operation getting my man back was starting to look bright.

Mega

After Hassan and I shot the shit for a lil bit I came back to my hotel room and thought about the shit he was spitting. I missed Dream's lil fiesty ass which is why I texted her. Baby was everything I wanted and needed but I wasn't with all that lying shit. I'm the last nigga she needs to lie to. I fuck with her the long way because up until that point shorty kept it a buck with me.

She had me feeling like shit was deeper than what she was insinuating. If the nigga was only a friend the fuck is she lying about it for? I read the text messages after the goofy broad kept sending message after message and I was tryna sleep. Shit was starting to piss me off. I ain't no hoe ass nigga that went through her phone on some let me see what she been up to. It was this broad texting her if she was layed up with her lame ass nigga which had me thinking.

I couldn't even tell you what even possessed Dream to even start fucking with some dyke bitch. I don't even know where ol girl came from. I thought it was a nigga the way they were texting back and forth but when Dream said she was only a friend that shit kinda bruised my muthafuckin' ego.

You know how crazy that shit sound? Ya girl textin another girl on some flirting shit. Like Dream's big headed ass was really into the shit. That shit had my mind gone. So yeah a nigga was lowkey in his feelings and I had to get from around her.

I was in New York for a bit but I was so tempted to hop on the highway and go check her, so I said fuck it and brought my ass down this way. I wasn't even sure what tip I was on because I wasn't interested in fucking with another bitch. I just wanted what was mine. After fuckin' with a real one you don't even want to fuck with anything else. I know what I have with Dream and I was willing to thug it out with her. Her type was rare.

She was poised yet outspoken. Crazy in a way, but sensible at the same time. She knew how to stay in her place and let me lead for the most part. I'm from New York and most of the bitches I encounter be on some real wild crazy shit, acting like niggas and that shit is super unattractive. Dream wasn't that. Yeah, she had her moments when her mouth was reckless but I ain't pay that no mind because at the end of the day she knew how to be a lady and I needed that.

She provided a peace that I couldn't get when I was out in the streets and that's the one thing I loved about her more than anything. At my age, I'm getting too old for all that extra shit anyways. I'm tryna settle down, invest in some shit and probably have a couple of bad ass kids running around and I wanted to do all of that with her.

But before I started planning our future and shit we had to make things right between the two of us.

****

Two Days Later

"What's the word bro?" I asked Hassan as I sat on the balcony of my hotel room at Conrad Miami enjoying the view of South Beach.

"Ain't shit. You still tryna buy Halima's part?" he asked me through the receiver.

"You already."

"Aight. Ima need you to slide through and sign some paperwork and shit. The sooner we get this shit done the quicker we can move on."

"Heard you."

"Aight. Ima be at the club in the next hour or so, so just hit my line if anything."

"Aight," I responded back to him as we disconnected the call.

Turning around and walking back into my room I grabbed my keys and a couple of other things I needed before heading out. The nigga said an hour or so. So by the time I finished getting something to eat I could make my way over to where he's at.

Once I made it to the lobby the place was busy. Muthafuckas was checking in and some checking out. I made a mental note to look into contacting a realtor. If I was gonna do business down here I was gonna need a more permanent situation. I wasn't with crowdy places. Shit made me uneasy.

Making my way down the walkway I prepared to take the short walk to the parking garage when I felt somebody bump into me and immediately it caused me to look down and I'll be damned if it wasn't the devil herself.

"Sorry. I wasn't watching where," she started to say but stopped once she saw me smirking down at her.

"Mega?"

"Wassup Dream?" I asked her as we looked in each other eyes.

"W-w-w-what are you, what are you doing here?"

"I should be asking you that little lady, you looking good."

"I-I-I-I came here with Satin."

"Calm down baby. Stop acting like you're nervous to see a nigga," I said with a chuckle as I played with her curls.

"What you doing walking out here by yourself anyways?"

"I wanted to sightsee, Satin is still asleep and I just wanted to get out the room for a bit," she said as she chewed on her bottom lip. A habit she had the tendency of doing whenever she got nervous.

"Where you staying?"

"Beach Park Hotel."

"Not too far from here, you want a ride? I can drop you off. I ain't doing shit."

"Mega, I don't know."

"I'm just dropping you off ma. Plus it's hot as fuck out here," I tried reasoning with her. I didn't realize I missed being in her presence until I locked eyes with her. One look at her and I forgot why I was even upset with her, to begin with. Aight maybe I'm lying but none of that shit mattered. She was here. In front of me. Looking stunning as usual.

Looking around at everyone walking around us she finally looked back at me then down to my hand that I had extended out for her before placing her hand into mine. This shit felt right. My mood had instantly shifted. And although we were walking hand in hand on a crowded busy strip I felt like it was just the two of us.

Finally reaching the black Mercedes Benz E- CLASS coupe I rented I opened the passenger door for her before going around to the driver side and getting in. Neither one of us said anything to the other for a few minutes. I guess we were both in our own thoughts and finally, I heard her soft voice call my name.

"Wassup?" I asked her glancing over at her momentarily before returning my attention on the road.

"I'm sorry," she said but I remained silent.

"I'm sorry for not telling you everything. I should've told you. But I swear to you I never did anything with her except kiss her. That's all. Nothing else happened and I should've told you when you asked. I was just scared. I was afraid that you would judge me."

"You like her?"

"No. I mean well yeah I had started to but I ended things. She was only supposed to be my friend. I'm not sure how we even got to where we were."

"Dream, I wasn't even mad that you was out entertaining some broad. I'm mad that you lied. I have never lied to you. Anything you wanted to know I kept it a buck with you and I wanted the same in return but you looked me in my eyes and deliberately lied to me. That's foul."

"And I said I was sorry. You have to believe me. I don't want her Mega, I want you," she confessed looking at me.

"Look," I said with a sigh as I pulled up to her hotel.

"If we gonna do this thing we gotta get some shit straight right now. I fuck with you because I adore the fuck outta you. It ain't just sex. It's you. As much as you piss me off sometimes I wouldn't trade you in for anyone else but moving forward I need you to have patience with me. I need to know that next time your little ass is feeling neglected that you ain't about to go do some dumb shit to fuck up what we have. I know you. That's why you were even entertaining it."

"I promise!"

"I'm dead ass Dream. I'm too grown for the back and forth. A nigga pushing 40 and shit. I'm working on a few things that can potentially secure our future, just relax a lil bit and trust me, aight?"

"I hear you."

"Nah it's either yes or no. You know your ass is hard headed."

"I'll trust you, okay?" she questioned as I grabbed the bottom of her face bringing her lips to mine, kissing her lightly before pulling away.

"Mega?"

"Sup?"

"I've missed you."

"I missed you too Dreamy," I told her and I meant it. A nigga world was feeling whole again.

Satin

You know I don't care bring that ass right her for me

Take it all off for me baby, lemme see somethin'

I know you the best for me, you're a real winner

Baby girl you bad as fuck, I'm a real nigga. You know

you know that I'll always be there for you. Won't let

you go, I'll always take care of you because you're

mine, pretty brown eyes

"You're my pretty brown eyess, they all on ya and they want youuu," I sung loudly as I looked through my suitcase for something to wear. It was 84 degrees and I was ready to snatch me up some nice eye candy today. I know I'm supposed to be helping Dream find Mega but I was going to have as much fun as possible because once I got back home it was down to business. I was starting school and ain't no telling when I'll be able to enjoy myself again.

Deciding on the coral colored maxi dress I slipped it on and matched it with a pair of gold sandals with matching gold stud earrings. It was too hot to wear my bundles down so I figured today I was going to wear it in a cute little bun on top of my head. I may be plus sized but I wasn't gonna be out here looking crazy. They won't have me going viral on Facebook.

As I started doing my hair the hotel room door opened and I knew it couldn't be anyone but Dream. When I woke up this afternoon I was alone and her hot ass was already gone. Where did she go? I have no idea. I'm assuming she couldn't go too far though because we didn't really know anyone out here except for Hassan and you already know I ain't fucking with him.

I will admit though I did miss the sex. He literally catered to every part of my body. The man wasn't shit but he was indeed a lover. Just the thought of him was causing my center to moist up a bit. I still can't believe things went down the way they did.

He wasn't my boyfriend so technically he didn't cheat so he wasn't guilty of that. He was, however, guilty of not being truthful and that shit was a dub. If I have to question anything that you say then we don't need to be around each other. Period. The only thing I hate more than a thief is a liar and he was that.

"Okayyyy big booty. Look at you!" Dream said all extra like as she came into the bathroom where I was and slapping me on my ass and I did a lil twerk.

"Why you gassin me?" I asked her with a laugh.

"I ain't gassin baby. You looking like a whole snack out here. You tryna bag somethin'?"

"You know I am. In the process of us tryna find yo man Ima be looking for one of these niggas to slut the fuck out!"

"About that.."

"Don't start ya shit Dream. You didn't bring me all the way down here for nothing. If you waste my time I just may need to put our friendship on ice."

"You're so dramatic."

"No, you are. You got us down here on a mission to find Mega."

"Bitch I saw him."

"Huh? How? Where?" I asked question after question as I stopped doing my hair and turning my attention to her.

"I saw him. I was walking by the beach downtown over by Brickwell and I accidentally bumped into someone and guess who it was?"

"Get the fuck outta here! Forreal?"

"Yupp!" she said with a cheesy ass smile.

"Okay don't get stingy now. Spill the tea bitch. What happened?"

"Nothing we were gazing into each other's eyes and we started talking, he dropped me off here."

"Okay, soooo what does that mean?"

"We good. I apologized and we decided to move past it. I got my man back bitch!"

"It's about damn time. I was tired of you crying. So y'all gonna see each other again while you down here?"

"Yeah, he actually invited us to some all white mansion party tonight."

"I don't have anything to wear."

"I got that covered. We going shopping."

"Dream, since you got his ass back, don't fuck up again tryna catch fish," I stated seriously.

"Hoe don't do me. I told you I'm not gay."

"That's what your mouth says, can't be too sure now."

"I swear I don't like you," she hissed and I giggled.

"That's fine because you loveeeee me!"

****

"Damnnn I wonder who lives here. This house is huge," I said to Dream as we both got out of the car Mega had sent for us.

Adjusting our outfits, we walked up to the house where we were granted access inside and it seemed like all eyes were on us. Dream was wearing this nice white Bondage type dress paired with a pair of royal blue pumps and her hair done in some loose curls done by yours truly. I, on the other hand, opted for a white jumpsuit that showed a little cleavage with a pair of gold stilettos. I decided to keep the bun just to show off my lovely cheekbones.

"Do I look alright? Do I have lipstick on my teeth? My titties don't look lopsided right?" Dream asked me as she looked around nervously.

"You look like you need a drink. Stop fidgeting like a damn crack head too. You making me nervous."

"It's just so many people here. You know my anxiety goes through the roof."

"Relax boo. You look good and when he sees you I'm almost sure you're going to take his breath away."

"You think so?"

"Dream yes girl. Relaxxxx," I told her again as a waiter stopped in front of us with a tray of champagne so I grabbed two handing one to Dream so she could calm her ass down a bit.

"I need to text Mega and let him know we made it."

"Thirsty much? We just got here. Give it a min."

"Satin you do see all these people here, right? He probably don't even think we made it yet."

"And? Let his ass come find you."

"That's why your ass is single. Playing all these damn games."

"Was that shade?" I asked her and she ignored me and texted away on her phone which was pointless because the moment I looked behind her he was walking our way with Hassan's ugly ass next to him.

"If it isn't the sexiest muthafucka in this bitch," he said into her ear causing her to blush.

"Wassup Satin?"

"Wassup Mega?"

"Satin, you can't speak?" Hassan asked me as he licked his lips.

"Hassan," I said keeping it short.

"Let me talk to you for a second."

"Uhhhh no."

"Satin, that's no way you treat someone when you're in their home."

"You live here?"

"That would be correct."

"WOW!" was all I could say. I knew Hassan had money but I didn't know he was caking like that.

"Are you gonna let me talk to you or are you going to continue to be stubborn?" he asked me and I decided to listen to what he had to say. Taking his hand, I followed him to the second floor and into what looked like to be game room, where there was a pool table and bar. As soon as we made it inside completely he closed the door and locked it behind him. He was looking fine as hell in his white linen suit and I knew being alone with him would be trouble. *Here goes nothing.* I thought to myself as he looked at me like I was his favorite meal and he was ready to eat.

Hassan

"How you been?" I asked Satin as I took in her appearance. She was looking good, too good to be exact.

"Great."

"You still mad?"

"You're kidding me, right?" she asked sarcastically but I didn't respond.

"Oh, you were serious. You lied to me and I'm supposed to not be mad? How does that work Hassan, huh?"

"I didn't lie to you."

"You didn't tell the truth either."

"I still didn't lie. I wasn't all the way honest with you."

"Sounds like lying to me."

"I didn't lie. I was waiting on the right time to tell you," I told her as I walked close enough to her that I could smell the mint on her breath.

"I apologize."

"I don't accept your apology."

"Why not? What I did wasn't that big of a deal."

"Maybe not to you but to me that changed our whole dynamic. You can't sit up here and tell me what is and isn't a big deal. You screwing multiple women is a big fucking deal."

"I wasn't sleeping with anyone when I was sleeping with you. I still haven't slept with anyone since you."

"I'm finding that hard to believe."

"It's the truth," I told her as I took the champagne glass out of her hand and setting it on the bar top.

"I've missed you," I whispered as I kissed her neck and surprisingly she didn't move away. Instead, a small moan escaped her mouth.

Satin was talking big shit but she knew what it was. She knew she wanted me just as bad as I wanted her. As I continued to suck and kiss on her neck I took my left hand and began caressing her breast through the thin fabric she was wearing. I had every intention on fucking Satin and showing her just how much I missed her. How much I needed her. Satin didn't know it but she had me hooked from the first time I ever laid eyes on her. That day when she walked through the foyer that time with her girls I knew there was something about her.

"Hassan," she moaned lowly as she looked at me through lust filled eyes and I brought my lips to hers and kissed her roughly as I continued to touch all over her. Unable to contain myself any longer I broke our kiss and quickly spun her around so that her back was now facing me and I took that as my opportunity to unzip the one piece she was wearing.

Undressing her slowly I licked her neck right as my free hand parted her thighs and I allowed my fingers to slide into her panties and into her lady part. As my index and middle finger worked her pussy, I took my thumb and played with her clit driving her crazy. She was so turned on that her pussy muscles began tightened around my fingers causing her sweet sugary juices to drip into my hand.

"Mmmmm Hassannnn. Yess. Oh yessss," she moaned as she took her hand and placed it on top of mine.

"Can I have you, Satin?" I whispered in her ear as I started finger fucking her faster.

"Hmmm? Can I have you sexy?"

"Mmmhmm!"

"Let me hear you say it, baby. Can I have you?"

"Yesss!"

"Yeah?"

"Yessss babbbbyyyy. Fuckkkkk," she continued to moan out and I removed my fingers, licking them.

Picking her up I carried her to where the pool table was and layed her down gently before kissing her soft lips again. I couldn't get enough of her and as much as I missed her I was trying my hardest not to rush this. My dick was pressing so hard against the pants that I was wearing. But I had to resist the urge to go in.

Kissing my way down her body I finally became face to face with the lace panties she was wearing and in one swift motion I had ripped them right off. Once they were removed I wasted no time in dipping my face in between her thick thighs and sucking on her sensitive bud as she ran her fingers through my hair. Her pussy was so wet that her juices was dripping unto my beard and I didn't even give a fuck. She could've flooded my shit and I wouldn't even care because she tasted so good.

"Mmmmm right thereeee," she cried lowly as she wrapped her legs around my neck.

"Yessss, oh yesss right there babyyyyyyy!"

"You taste.. So.. Fuckin'.. Good ma," I said into her pussy in between licks.

"Cum for me sexy," I said as I looked up into her eyes with my mouth still latched on to what had become my favorite meal, her pussy.

"Shiiiiiiitttttttttttt Hassan. Don't stop. Don't stooooppppppppp!"

"You gon' cum for me?" I asked her and she just began grinding her box deeper into my mouth.

"Just.. Like.. Thatttttttttt. Fuckkkkk. Oh my goddddddddd," she panted as she came in my mouth allowing me to slurp up all of her juices.

Standing up I took a look at the beautiful woman in front of me and I wanted her to feel me. Like really feel me. She been playing this entire time but it was time to let Satin know that daddy was home and she had no choice but to deal with it.

Satin

After the tongue lashing Hassan had just put on me I couldn't even think clearly. I was supposed to mad at him for what happened yet all I could do was look at him through hazy vision with pure lust. The kisses and licks he had placed on my hot pocket were soft and oh so gentle. They felt so good that I almost forgot why I was upset in the first place.

Grabbing me by my waist and pulling me towards him with so much force and intensity I let a small moan escape my full lips as I smiled up at him. *Showtime.* I thought to myself as he rubbed his dick up and down my opening teasing my clit. I didn't want to be teased. I wanted and needed to be fucked. I wanted him to fuck me as if someone was watching and we were putting on a show and I guess in a sense we were. Here he was hosting a party with a house filled with partygoers yet he had managed to escape to give me something that we both were missing.

Finally feeling him making way into my *kitty kat* I moaned as that first poke spoke to my soul. That shit felt so fucking good that if I could, I would have that over and over again. As he gave my body slow and gentle strokes my body purred beneath him. As he continued to cater to my body I felt myself get wetter and wetter with every stroke.

I just gazed into his eyes as he kept slipping and sliding in my walls as I heard the DJ outside change the song to Chris Brown's Hope You Do. Taking my hands I pressed them firmly against his chest as he began picking up his pace hitting every spot imaginable inside of my goodies and I swear he felt so fucking good. I wanted this to last forever. No words were spoken as he pounded into me. The only thing that could be heard was skin slapping, our moans mixed in with Chris Brown's singing.

And she know I'm gon lay the pipe, pipe down. I turn that bitch crazy

Why you trippin'? You won't even listen cause you used to all the niggas

I promise I'm different. And I hope you take your clothes off, know I'm

persistent, I know that ass is soft.

"You better not nut yet either," I ordered as I tightened my pussy muscles around his dick.

"Fuckkkkkk," he groaned as he slowed his pace down and I immediately scooted back. I meant what I said. I didn't want him to cum just yet. I didn't want him to cum until I was ready for him to.

Getting on all fours I crawled to him and placed a sloppy kiss on his lips as I grabbed a fistful of the little bit of hair he had on his head. Taking my tongue I licked his lips and smiled a devious smile when we both locked eyes with one another.

"Lay down," I said seductively patting the spot next to me on the pool table.

"Satin. what you tryna do ma?" he asked as he tried going in for a kiss but I put my hand up.

"Lay down first," I told him with much authority in my voice and he finally obliged.

"What type of time are you on Satin?" he asked me as he layed on the pool table and I ignored him. Instead, I searched with my eyes for something to tie his hands with and I finally found my lace panties on the floor.

Getting down from on top of the pool table I grabbed my ripped panties before climbing back onto the table and straddling him.

"You trust me?" I asked him with one of my eyebrows arched.

"Satin.."

"Do. You. Trust. Me?" I asked him again waiting on him to answer.

"Yeah man, I trust you," he finally said and I smiled showing off my dimples. Grabbing both his wrist I took the panties and tied them tightly around his wrist and the look of horror was etched all across his face causing me to giggle a little.

"Fuck is you doing?"

"Nothing yet," I told him as I got on top of him in a squatting position.

"Yesssssss," I hissed as I rocked my hips back and forth slowly before sliding up and down his stick. Taking my hands and placing them on his bondaged ones I was enjoying feeling every inch of him as a sucked him in deeper with my pussy as if it was a suction cup.

"Fuck girl," he groaned as his face contorted in some ugly ass way and as weird as this is about to sound I could've came right then and there off that face alone so I decided to spin around with his dick still planted inside of me.

Taking my hands I held on to his ankles as I bounced my ass up and down giving him a nice little view of my round voluptuous ass and from the sound of things it was driving him crazy. My pussy was so fucking wet you could literally hear it. As my head fell back my eyes rolled to back as my mouth was slightly opened. I was on the verge of cumming and I wanted him to cum with me.

"Hassannnnn fuckkkk this dick feels so fucking goodddd," I moaned loudly as I felt his dick jump inside of my pussy.

"That's right. Cum for me. Cum for me all in this pussy."

"Shitttt," he groaned lowly and I began squeezing my muscles around him tightly landing on him hard. I was putting in work. I needed this.

"Oh gawddddd I'm about to.. cummmmmmmmm," I cried as I felt him spill his seeds into me at the same time. Once we both had come to the only thing that could be heard was panting from the both of us.

Finally getting from up off of him I untied his hands and tried to move away but he pulled me into him and just looked at me with so much passion that it was almost scary. I didn't want to feel what I thought I was feeling for him. Hassan didn't deserve my heart but I just fucked him like he did.

"Satin, I want this," he confessed and I didn't say anything I just continued to look at him in a dumbfounded way. I was stuck. I didn't know what to say so I didn't say anything.

****

After Hassan and I little sex session I quickly gathered my things and got the hell out of there. My hair was a mess and my makeup was a mess so there was absolutely no way I could stay around and partake in the party. I sent Dream a text letting her know I was going back to the hotel room and she let me know she was staying with Mega for the night so here I was just laying in bed deep into my thoughts.

I wasn't sure what I wanted to do with Hassan. I mean yeah we just had some mind-blowing sex but that doesn't change the fact that he's all about poly life and that's something I just couldn't get with it. You have to be one weak and desperate bitch to even consider that shit granted, I'm not judging women who actually partake in that lifestyle but that's my opinion. I just couldn't make sense of it and trust me I tried to.

Anyways he and I had alot of chemistry and sexually we were very much compatible but if we were to give each other a fair chance he would have to make me his one and only. I wasn't accepting anything less from him. Fuck his wealth, well not really but shit rich or not I wasn't compromising. PERIOD!

Turning over my phone chimed with a notification just as there was a knock at the door. Getting up to answer it my phone began ringing. Glancing at the phone I saw that it was Isabella and I made a mental note to call her back. Opening the door my voice got stuck in my throat as I looked at Hassan but before he could day anything my phone rang again and it was Isabella. Holding my finger up I answered her call.

"Hey, Iz-" I started to say but she cut me off.

"Satin you need to come home!" she said hysterically into the phone.

"Hold on Izzy. Calm down. What's wrong?"

"Satin please just come home."

"Izzy, what's wrong? What happened?"

"Satin, I don't.. I don't.. I don't.. Fuck just come home!" she demanded again.

"Iz, you're scaring me. What's wrong? Just spit it out."

"I don't know how to say this but uh it's Kori. She's umm.. She's," she said but she was beginning to piss me off.

"Dammit, Izzy just fucking say it already. What's wrong with Kori?"

"Satin, she's, she's gone."

"She's what? Gone like missing right?"

"She's dead Satin," Izzy said and I instantly felt sick to my stomach. Letting the phone slip out of my hand I released a gut-wrenching scream and Hassan immediately caught me just as my knees buckled.

I couldn't do anything but cry. I was at a loss for words. How did this happen? Why did this happen? Did she kill herself. The more I thought about how things had been between the two of us I felt like shit. I should've been the bigger person. I should've reached out. I should've told her I loved her. The harder I cried the tighter Hassan held onto me and in that moment I was so thankful for him being there.

Isabella

I was so close to having a mental breakdown. Between working in the ER and seeing Kori being brought in on a stretcher then having the police do a health and wellness check on Joi because she refused to take my calls. I even went by her place but since she changed her locks I no longer had a spare key. I wasn't sure what was going on. I felt like somebody was playing a sick ass joke on us and I wasn't here for it. I just don't understand why there was such a black cloud over us.

Thankfully Joi was okay according to the police but Kori sadly met her demise. My heart was broken and I couldn't help but think Jacob somehow had something to do with both of these ladies being in the situation that they found themselves in. Shit is really fucked up and life as we all knew it had changed drastically in a blink of an eye.

"Bae, you need to relax," Sincere said to me as he sat next to me handing me a cup of hot ginger tea.

"Sin.. I love you. I swear I do. I love you a little more today then I did yesterday. I don't know what I would do if I ever lost you," I cried.

"Shhh, baby I ain't going nowhere. Calm down."

"No. You need to hear this. I know I'm not always fair to you but I love you. I may not show you all the time but I'm forever thankful for you. I can't imagine life without you. I don't even care that you've been hiding my birth control pills. If you want babies I'll give you as many as you like I just don't want to fight. I don't want to lose sight of what's important. Life is short and I don't want to spend another minute being ungrateful or holding grudges. I just can't," I continued to cry and he just looked at me with this sympathetic look.

"Bell.."

"I don't even care Sincere. I don't. I don't want to fight with you about it. I don't want to argue about it. We don't even have to talk about it. It's stupid. I have way too much going on and I don't want to stress about stupid things."

"You got it," he said pulling me into him.

At first, I was upset about him hiding the pills but with everything else going on I honestly didn't even care. I had other issues to worry about. Life was bigger than those dumb ass pills. They were making me crazy anyways so he kind of did me a favor. I just hate that he felt like he couldn't just come and talk to me about us having children. I was feeling like he was tryna trap me but I didn't want to fight about it, especially not right now. Not with all this weird shit going on.

Life was way too short and I didn't want to let it pass me by because I was too busy being angry. Because I was being unappreciative.

****

Satin and Dream had finally made it back home and I was currently waiting on them at Joi's house so that we could try to get in touch with her. For the past six years, all I knew was them and if one was going through something that meant we all were going through something. That's just how we rolled. Wasn't no dealing with anything on our own so I was truly worried that something was up with Joi.

Looking through my rearview mirror I saw that Satin and Dream had arrived so I shut my car off and got out as I waited for them to do the same. As soon as Satin got out I noticed that she looked like shit. She was taking Kori's death hard and it showed. Where there has always been a smile on her face was now replaced with a somber expression. Dream, on the other hand, looked like she was glowing and after figuring out what was going on with Joi I was going to ask her about Miami.

"Hey," I spoke to them as they reached me.

"Hey you," Dream responded.

"Hey," Satin said keeping it short.

"Y'all ready? If she doesn't open up the door I think we should break a window or something. I'm not leaving until we get in touch with her," I told them and they agreed.

As we made our way to the door silence filled the air. Preparing to knock on the door I heard Joi's voice.

"It's open," she said from the other side of the door. Opening it I took one look at her and knew something was wrong.

"Why haven't you been answering our calls?" Dream asked her cutting straight to the chase.

"Right. We've been worried sick. That's not like you to go MIA for this long," I chimed in as we all took a seat in the living room. Joi just burst into tears.

"What's wrong?" I asked her getting closer to her.

"Jacob. He raped me. That light skinned muthafucka raped me," she revealed and we were all speechless.

"What you mean he raped you?" Dream asked as she stood up and began pacing the floor.

"He forced me to have sex with him. I never felt so low and dirty in my life. My husband raped me. RAPED ME!" she yelled with tears still falling down her eyes.

"You need to tell the police, Joi. You can't let him get away with that."

"Tell the police what? That the man I exchanged vows with turned into someone I don't even recognize and had sex with me that I didn't consent to? There's no evidence. It'll be his word against mine. The police ain't gonna do a damn thing. Fuck them."

"You should still-," I tried to say but she threw a glass at the front door causing glass to shatter everywhere before yelling.

"ISABELLA JUST STOP! SHUT THE FUCK UP FOR A MOMENT. FOR ONCE STOP BEING NIAVE. THE POLICE DON'T GIVE A FUCK ABOUT US."

"REALLY JOI? I COME TO CHECK ON YOU AND YOU YELL AT ME LIKE I'M THE FUCKING ENEMY. SCREW YOU!"

"I DIDN'T ASK FOR YOU TO BE HERE. YOU CAN GO! I WAS FINE. I WAS FINE BEFORE Y'ALL CARRIED Y'ALL NOSEY ASSES OVER HERE. I WANTED TO BE ALONE!"

"I don't have to deal with this shit. I've been quiet this entire time but you need to stop being so damn ungrateful. My fucking cousin is dead and you sitting up here mad at the fucking universe cussing everyone out," Satin finally spoke and Joi looked at her with her eyebrows knitted together.

"Cousin? Who Kori?" Joi asked surprised.

"Bitch who else?"

"Satin.." Dream said to Satin giving her a saddened look.

"Don't Satin me. Y'all over here trying to be a good friend to her meanwhile she's chewing y'all fucking heads off. Shit is disrespectful and ungrateful as fuck. Muthafuckas took time out of their day to come check on her."

"Kori is dead?" Joi asked again.

"W-w-w-hat? How?"

"Police said someone killed her. I don't have to be here Joi. WE don't have to be here. Bitches been worried sick about you yet you over here acting like we're you're enemy when we're not. I'm sorry Jacob did what he did but I would think instead of lashing out on the people who love you the most that you would lean on them for comfort," Satin responded to her as she tried to fight her tears but it didn't work. Her tears fell anyway.

"I gotta go," she said as she stood to leave.

"Satin you're in no condition to drive," Dream tried to reason with her.

"How did we get here?" Joi asked out loud but we didn't say anything. Hell, I was trying to figure out the same thing.

We went from having a great and amazing bond to this. Nobody expected this. Things were bad and nobody knew how to cope with it. We were all affected by everything that has transpired and now wasn't the time to go against one another. We needed to unite but judging by Joi's outburst and Satin's withdrawal I wasn't sure when things were going to get better for us.

Dream

Two Weeks Later

I was currently at home preparing dinner as I counted down the hours until I saw my baby again. I was missing him something crazy and all I wanted to do was be wrapped up in his arms. So much has been going on that I just wanted to feel a sense a peace and I've only felt that when I'm around him. Crazy how you can go your whole life missing something and not realizing how essential it is until you have the pleasure of experiencing it. Especially after hearing about Kori and Joi I couldn't wait to just love up on him and cherish him as long as I'm able to.

It had been a few weeks since we found out about Kori's death and the police had no leads on who committed the act. My heart was hurting for Satin. This girl had her grandmother in a nursing home and she had to bury her cousin. Baby couldn't catch a break to save her life still she pushed through and gave Kori a beautiful homegoing service. I admired her strength.

Joi was still acting distant with us so I fell back and just decided to just let her go through what she was going through. At the end of the day, I understood where she was coming from to an extent because after losing my mother I didn't want to deal with anyone. So yes I understood what it felt like to go through something and having people who couldn't relate to that same pain. I've never been violated in that way so I didn't know what that felt like, however, I did know pain. I was close to asking Mega to handle Jacob. You don't do no bullshit like that and think you're going to have good luck. Nah, that's not how the world operates.

As far as Mega goes, everything between the two of us was cool. After we talked and made up we haven't had problems of any sort. Maybe we were in our little honeymoon stage but regardless of anything that happens whether it's good or bad I had plans on sticking through it with him and working it out. There wasn't even no point in denying it anymore, the man had my heart and all I could do at this point was hope and pray that he didn't break it.

Turning the stuffed shells I had cooking in the oven on low, I walked around my apartment and began lighting candles. I was going to make sure that tonight would be a night Mega would never forget. I had bought a bottle of his favorite champagne. Made his favorite dish and even bought some sexy lace lingerie to model in for him. I wanted to make tonight special just for him.

I was already showered so the only thing left for me to do was to do my makeup and hair. There was no way I was looking basic tonight. Any other time, I'm probably regular as hell but because I wanted to show him the reason why he chose me in the first place I had to pull out all the shots. I had to come correct or not come at all.

After about an hour or so I was finally done with getting myself together and I looked at my reflection in the floor length mirror. I had to admit that I looked good. The Thrill Me Lace lingerie set I ordered from Fashion Nova fit my body like a glove and I was sure that I had made the right decision when I ordered it. The lingerie set tied in with what I did to my hair and makeup had me looking like something you'd put on a silver platter. You hear me? A bitch was looking bomb as fuck.

Before heading to the kitchen I checked my phone to see if anyone had sent me a text but there was no notifications so I paired my phone to the Bluetooth speaker I had and turned some music on before I began preparing the table. I was a nervous wreck. I know I shouldn't be seeing as though Mega isn't a new guy but I just wanted to make sure things were perfect. He deserved nothing less than that.

Once I was done getting everything together I sat at the table nursing a glass of wine just waiting until he walked through the door and I couldn't help but smile to myself. I never thought we'd be here. When we met I thought we would hook up a couple of times and eventually things would fade away. You know how things or situationships are nowadays. Y'all meet, hookup a few times then eventually things just end. It's like an unspoken mutual agreement the two of you make. But that didn't happen with us. I thought it would but it didn't.

Yeah, I did a bunch of stupid things in the process but my heart couldn't deny the fact that this man was who it wanted. That whole Sosa situation shouldn't even had happened but it did and I paid for that. My curiosity got the best of me and for a while there it was winning until reality slapped me in the face.

I was soooo stupid for that. Why did you even let me play myself like that? Matter of fact why did Satin and the girls let me play myself like that? I was bold and wild as fuck for that. Honestly, I was.

Finally hearing a set of keys jingle I took another sip and sat up straight as I looked straight ahead to my front door waiting to see him walk in. I had all the lights off with only the candles lit as my playlist played on low. The moment he stepped foot into the apartment he began calling my name not realizing I was sitting within his view the entire time.

"Dream?" Mega called out to me but I didn't answer. Dropping his bags at the door he went to take a left into the living room but he noticed me. He stopped midway and brought his fist to his mouth before biting it.

"Dreamy?"

"Who else would it be?" I asked him in a seductive tone.

"You look good. You look amazing!"

"Thank you. I figured my man would love it."

"He must be a lucky ass nigga if you did all of this. I'm jealous."

"Jealous huh? That's a first."

"Yeah, I mean he gotta be a lucky ass muthafucka. He got your lil fiesty ass bringing out all the tricks," he said finally making his way to me and picking me up. Wrapping my arms around his neck I placed a soft and gentle kiss on his lips before smiling.

"If I had to say so myself I'd definitely say I was the lucky one."

"Word?"

"Yeah. How could I not be? You're amazing," I cooed as I looked into his hazel eyes.

"I ain't all that. I'm just a regular ass nigga. I just be coolin' baby."

"Regular or not you're amazing to me."

"Preciate it. I think right now though, I'm the lucky one. Look at this. You got this sexy ass shit on, some muthafuckin' candles lit, table set. Shit official as fuck ma," he said as he caressed my little booty.

"You hungry? I made your fav. Stuffed shells, salad and garlic cheesy bread."

"I got an appetite for something else."

"Why you gotta be nasty?"

"I walk up in this bitch and you sitting at the table looking good as fuck and you wondering why I'm being nasty? I'm tryna see if you taste as good as you looking right now."

"Eat first and then we can do whatever you like. Now let me go," I told him but he didn't listen.

"I swear Mega, ya greedy ass eat fast as hell so you can wait 15, 20 minutes." I fussed and he finally let me go.

"Thank you!"

Walking over to the oven I took the food out and made our plates. After I had finally finished doing that I sat his plate down in front of him and poured him a glass of Dom Perignon before walking over to the opposite side of the table and taking a seat.

"This is good baby," Mega complimented me as he chewed on his food.

"Thanks, bae. So, how was your flight?"

"It was cool. Soon I won't be flying back and forth as much. I'm thinkin' about moving out there."

"M-m-move out where?" I asked choking on my Chardonnay.

"Miami. Hassan and I doing business together. I can't keep an eye on things from up here ma. Ima have to leave."

"But, what about us?"

"You coming with me, fuck you thought?"

"Mega, I can't just leave."

"Why not?" he asked putting his fork down, sitting back in his seat looking at me.

"My life is here. My friends. My job. My apartment. I can't just leave."

"Dream, you trust me, right?"

"Of course I do. You know that."

"So why can't you trust me with this move? Eventually, you're going to have to grow up and leave your friends. You don't want to leave because everything is familiar and they're probably your security blanket but at some point, you gotta put you first. Put your happiness first, you hear me?"

"I hear you but.. I don't know."

"Look," he said with a sigh.

"I see a future with you. If I didn't I wouldn't have proposed the idea of you moving down there with me. We can buy a house. Fuck this apartment. We'll buy brand new shit. You can start your own business or something or take your degree with you. Baby all I need is a yes or no. That's it. You gonna let ya man lead this time or you gonna let this shit stop us from moving forward with our life together. I'm tryna see you barefoot and pregnant. I don't want much. Just trust me," he pleaded and I didn't even have to think twice about what I was about to do.

Getting up and walking over to him I extended my hand out to him taking it into mine I led him to my bedroom where I had more candles lit as well as a glass of Black Label which was another one of his faves. Helping him out of his clothing, I undressed him as our eyes never left one another's. Once we were done I handed him the glass and told him to lay on his stomach so that I could give him a massage.

"All of this for me?" he asked laying on his tattooed stomach.

"Of course," I told him straddling his back and pouring some oil into the palm of my hands. Starting at his shoulders I rubbed the oil in and worked my magic as he released a groan.

"Can I tell you something?"

"Go head"

"You remember the first time we met?"

"Yeah, you and Satin wasn't paying attention where y'all were going and I almost ran y'all asses the fuck over."

"I was gonna sue you too," I responded laughing.

"Y'all was jaywalking. You wasn't winning that case Dreamy," he responded with a chuckle.

"Says who? Nigga this ain't New York. Who says jaywalking? Nah seriously, when you jumped out the car I was so captivated and didn't give a damn about you almost hitting us. I wanted you then but you made sure we were okay and drove away. I didn't think we would meet again but we did at bum ass Wendy's and fate had its way. That was what? Eight, nine months ago? Who would've thought we would be here?"

"Life has a funny way of working things out," he said turning over causing me to fall next to him.

"Really Mega? I'm tryna be all romantic and you ruining it."

"You talkin' too much. I don't want to talk."

"Is that so?" I asked licking my lips and positioning myself in between his legs just as H.E.R. Every Kind Of Way started playing. Pulling on his briefs he lifted up his hips a little to help me remove them. As I listened to her voice sing through the speakers I took his massive dick and began stroking it with both of my hands.

This ain't a dream, you're here with me. Boy, it don't get no better

than you. For you, I wanna take my time all night. I wanna love you in

every kind of way. I wanna please you, no matter how long it takes. If

the world should end tomorrow and we only have today. I'm gonna love

you in every kind of way. Give you all, give you all of me when you need

it 'cause I need it. I wanna fall like your favorite season.

Looking up into his eyes as I continued to stroke him slowly I took my tongue and teased the tip of his thick mushroom head never stopping the hand job I was giving him.

"Dream why you playing with me?" he asked in a low raspy voice.

Ignoring him I stopped stoking him with my hands and took my tongue and licked up and down the shaft with my eyes still trained on him. The look of pleasure on his face was making my pussy wet. Taking my left hand I rubbed my clit through the thin fabric I was wearing as I inched his dick into my mouth.

Relaxing my throat muscles I deep throated him like my life depended on it and the more he groaned the more I got turned on. I was slurping on his stick with so much precision and skill that he couldn't handle it. He was trying his hardest to pull me up by my hair but I wasn't letting up. I just kept sucking.

"DREAM! MOVE MA!" Mega said loudly in a frustrated tone still I wouldn't stop. I knew he was about to cum and I wanted him to, right in my mouth. I was drinking babies and all tonight. After a few more minutes of hearing him cursing underneath his breath he relaxed and shot his load right down my throat and I swallowed every last drop.

Once he was finished I got up with a smile on my face and he pulled me to him and gave me one of the wettest and sloppiest kiss he has ever given me.

"Turn that ass over!" he demanded and I did just as I was told.

Getting on all fours I had my ass straight in the air with my face buried into my mattress and in a matter of seconds Mega had ripped the thong I was wearing and was ripping into my opening with so much force that I cried out to the angels.

"Gooooooooood!" I moaned

"Shut up!" he said slapping me on the ass as he continued to slide in and out of me.

"Mmmmmm!"

"Shit Dream!"

"Fuckkkkk babyyyy. Fuck meeeeee!"

"This my pussy Dreamy? Hmm?"

"Yessss. Oh, fuck yesssss. It's yours. It's all yourssss. Shittt I think I, I think I lovee youu!"

Biting down onto my lip to keep from moaning my eyes began to roll to the back of my head. Mega was fucking the shit out of me. He was taking out all of his frustrations on my pussy and I didn't mind it one bit. Reaching his hand around to my clit he began applying pressure on it and I bout lost my mind. He wasn't playing fair. I couldn't hold out much longer.

"Meeeeeggggggaaaaaaaa oh fuckkkk I'm about to cummmmmmm," I cried.

"Cum on your dick then," he coached and bitch he ain't have to tell me twice. Before I knew it my toes began to curl and my pussy muscles squeezed onto him causing me to cum hard. Grabbing a fistful of my hair he yanked my head back kissing my lips as he came again for the second time.

"I love you too Dreamy."

I was happy. He was happy. WE were happy and I couldn't ask for anything more.

Joi

"Who the hell is banging on my damn this late?" I asked out loud glancing at the clock on my wall.

It was way past midnight yet somebody was banging on my damn door this late. I still wasn't in the mood to be bothered with anyone. Whoever was on the other side of the door better have a damn good excuse on why they're here.

Reaching the door I unlocked it and swung it open without asking who it was. I was trippin cause it could've been anyone but I didn't care. At this point nothing scared me and if it was Jacob's ass this time I was prepared. I had something for him this time around but to my surprise, it was the police on the other side of my door.

"Ma'am, are you Mrs. Joi Bradley?" One of the officers asked me.

"Yes, sir I am. How may I help you?" I asked now concerned.

"Sorry for us being here so late but is there a way that we could come in?"

"Sure," I told them and moved to the side allowing them access into my home.

"Feel free to have a seat."

"Thank you, ma'am," the other officer said and they both took a seat next to each other.

"May I ask why you all are here this late?"

"Uh, do you know a Jacob Bradley?" the first officer asked me and I rolled my eyes.

"Yes, sir I do. Unfortunately, he's my husband."

"I'm not sure how to say this but we were called in for a disruption of peace at a nearby motel and your husband was staying at."

"Okay, I'm not following. What does that have to do with me?" I asked with an attitude. I didn't give a damn about what Jacob had going on.

"Your husband, he was.. he was found dead. An apparent suicide," the second officer said and I went numb. I didn't know how to feel. I heard what he just said but I was having a hard time trying to process it all.

"I'm sorry to have to spring all of this on you at this hour but we need you to go down to the morgue and identify the body."

"Um.. O-o-okay," I managed to get out.

"Sorry to have to be the barrier of bad news," one said standing up as the other followed suit.

"So sorry for your loss ma'am," they both said as I walked them to the door. Going back to couch I sat down and just stared off into space.

Jacob was dead. After all the shit he put me through he was gone. I know they said that I needed to go down and identify his body but to be honest I had no desire to. He hurt me to the core and his true colors showed himself when he came over and took what didn't belong to him.

I had no remorse in my heart for what he had done to himself. I didn't care. Without even realizing it I had began crying. And before you ask how could I cry over someone who hurt me the way he did I wasn't crying tears of sadness. I was crying tears of joy. No, I probably shouldn't be celebrating his death but for the first time in my life, I felt something I hadn't felt since I was in my younger years. I felt freedom. In some crazy way, his death had set me free.

****

"Thank you for meeting me," I said to Satin as we sat down at a table down at Tower Square downtown on Main street.

"No problem," she responded keeping it short.

"How you holding up?"

"I'm okay. Every day gets easier to deal with. I heard about what happened to Jacob. How are you feeling?"

"Can I be completely honest with you?" I asked her and she nodded her head yes.

"I feel fine. Is that weird? When the police delivered the news I wasn't sure how to feel. I was just numb to it but once I let it marinate a little bit I felt like a weight had been lifted off of my shoulders. I felt free. Satin the first time in twelve years I felt free."

"It's not weird. He broke you down and hurt you more than anyone probably will ever hurt you so no it isn't weird."

"I mean I have my moments when I wonder why. But I quickly shake those thoughts out my head because everything happens for a reason. At least that's what I was told. My heart hurts when I think about this baby I'm carrying because it wasn't conceived out of love but it's still mine."

Yup, you read that right, I'm pregnant. I wasn't feeling well and once I thought about the last time I had a period I carried myself down to the doctors and they confirmed what I had already suspected. When my midwife told me I was pregnant I cried in her office. I was so angry. I didn't want this child but there was absolutely no way that I would get rid of it. I somehow someway was going to figure out how to accept this child.

"Wait, you're pregnant? How?" she asked and I shot her a knowingly look and she grabbed my hand.

"Oh Joi, I'm sorry. Are you going to go through with this pregnancy?"

"Yes, as crazy as it may seem I am," I told her and she squeezed on my hand.

"I'll be fine Sat. I didn't overcome all of this just to give up. Besides, maybe this baby was meant to happen. The circumstances are fucked up but still, it happened and it happened for a reason."

"You're not worried? Scared? This baby can remind you of all things bad."

"This is true but it can also turn out to be something beautiful. Jacob is no longer here, he can't hurt me anymore. This baby is kinda like a fresh start although it has his DNA. I can't explain it but I'm keeping it."

"You don't owe me any explanations. If this is what you want to do then as your friend I'm going to support you. That's what friends do."

"Thank you, Satin. You have no idea how much that means to me."

"Whew! You're having a baby and Izzy is getting married. I wonder what's next," Satin joked.

"Crazy how the stars align ain't it?"

"Girllll tell me about it," we both laughed and it felt good. We both were going through our pain yet we still managed to smile because in spite of everything life was beautiful and there was so much to smile about.

Satin

I had every intention on asking Joi about what Kori had written in the letter she had left me. I had finally gotten around to opening that envelope she had left me and she elaborated on that messy situation she had created. She also gave me some information about my mother which is why I was on my way to the other side of town to meet her. I had some questions and according to Kori, she had all the answers.

I was so tired of secrets. It seemed like everyone around me had something to hide and I was so sick of it. I wouldn't even care if these secrets they tried so hard to bury didn't resurface. The entire time I was reading the letter I was shaking. I was mad. Mad as hell to be exact.

Pulling up to this bungalow style house I turned my car off and said a quick prayer before exiting. Making my way up the brick walkway I finally made it to the door and before I got a chance to press the doorbell, Renee, my mother had already opened it for me.

"Thank you for coming, come in," she said sweetly yet nervous at the same time.

Walking in I looked around and took note of how beautifully it was decorated. The house was very modern and chic. She looked to be doing well for herself and I caught myself feeling a little envious of the other children she had went on to have.

"Impressive," I said and she smiled.

"Have a seat. You want something to drink?"

"No thank you, I'm fine."

"Satin, you don't have to be so tense. I'm your mother," she said reaching for me but I moved.

"My mother wouldn't have left me"

"I apologized for that. What more do you want from me? I can't undo what's already been done. I'm here now. That has to count for something. I'm here. I'm trying to be a part of your life but it's up to you to let me be Satin."

"How do I know I can trust you? How do I know you're not going to leave again? Your mother took care of me when you were fully capable of doing that yourself."

"Satin, baby I can't go back in time and change things. I was young when I had you. I wasn't ready to be anyones mother. I was selfish. I made the best decision I could have possibly made when it came to you. You were safe and well taken care of and that's all that mattered to me."

"What about Kori?" I asked her handing her the letter and she looked like she saw a ghost.

"That boy has always been a pain in my ass," she said with a long drawn out sigh.

"Have a seat Satin, please," she pleaded and I took a seat opposite of hers.

"I had him three years before you. I didn't want him so I signed all my rights over to mama. I couldn't deal with looking into a child's eye who was the product of rape. I couldn't do it. I didn't want to relive those memories every time I looked at him in his eyes. It was mamas fault so I gave him to her. She knew that her brother had a thing for little girls. I tried telling her one time and she ignored me. So, of course, the abuse continued to happen and it went on until I had Kori."

I was speechless. I wasn't expecting to hear all of that. Kori was my brother? Well, sister. I knew we resembled each other a little but I just thought it was strong genes. The more I thought about it the more I understood why she gave him up but why give me up? Why not stick around and try to take care of me? All my life all I wanted was my mother. I often found myself wondering what her favorite food was. Or what our relationship would be like. It was those little moments I wanted to experience with her that I would never be able to do.

"Satin?" she called me taking me out of my thoughts.

"Hmm?"

"I'm sorry. I know it won't change anything but I'm sorry and I'm willing to spend the rest of my life making it up to you."

"Baby steps," I told her looking into her eyes.

"Understood," she said as she gave me a half smile.

My mind was blown. When you think you have things all figured out, life throws another curve ball and I was ready to go.

"Satin, I thought about you-," she began saying just as my phone started ringing.

"It's the nursing home, I have to take this," I told her getting up and taking the call in the hallway. With every word that the nurse on the other end of the phone spoke, I couldn't help but prepare myself for the worst. Once we disconnected our call I told Renee that grandma had been rushed to the hospital due to her being unresponsive.

I was too out of it to drive so we took her car and the quick 10-minute drive to the hospital felt like 30 minutes and the entire time I knew in my heart my grandmother wasn't going to make it. I felt it. An overwhelming feeling came over me and I released a gut-wrenching cry. I couldn't explain it but I knew. I knew she was gone.

****

The day had come for me to lay my grandmother to rest and as I sat in the first row of our church looking at her casket I was numb. Lost almost. What was I supposed to do without her? I still couldn't believe she was no longer with me. And I hated God for taking her from me. What did I do to deserve so much loss?

It turns out grandmother suffered a stroke and it was just too much stress on her body and she didn't make it. I showed my ass at that hospital that day and surprisingly I found comfort in Renee. Even now as I sit here drowning in emotions she's sitting to the left of me holding my hand as she too mourns. Now I understood what grams meant when she said we would need each other. She knew her time was coming to an end but as I always I didn't take her seriously. I had it in my mind that she would live forever.

I will say though, my grandmother was loved. The church was filled with everyone whose life she had touched over the years. I've received so many condolences from everyone that I just wanted them to stop. I wanted them to stop telling me that everything would get better. Or that she's in a better place. I was tired of hearing it. I honestly didn't want to be here right now but here I was listening to the church choir sing my grandmother's favorite gospel song by James Fortune.

Even though I can't see and I can't feel your touch. I will trust you, Lord. How I love you so much. Though the nights may seem

long and I feel so alone, lord my trust is in you. I surrender to you.

I just silently cried as they sung and I felt someone sit beside me wrapping their arms around me causing me to look up and it was Hassan. I hadn't spoken to him much since I left Miami but here he was in the flesh looking at me with so much compassion and sympathy. He always had the habit of showing up whenever I was going through something. It's like he knew I was going through something and I needed him. As if he was in tune with me.

Taking my right hand he brought it to his lips and kissed the back of it and I couldn't help but smile through my tears. After all the frogs I've kissed he was the one. He had to be. I was taking my grandmother's last piece of advice and I was letting my guard down. I was going to let my prince charming rescue me and Hassan was that for me.

Isabella

Eighteen Months Later

"Izzy stay still," Dream fussed at me as she fluffed the bottom of my dress. Today was the day. I was officially getting married and I couldn't wait. Words couldn't describe the way that I was feeling.

"I can't help it. I'm anxious," I said as I looked at myself in the mirror.

"Satin, Oh My Godddd," I went on to gush as I admired my makeup and the halo braid she had done to my hair.

"You like?" she asked me and I turned around so fast that I almost caught whiplash.

"Like? Bitch I love it! I look so, so, so angelic."

"Whew! I thought she was about to say pure. I was gonna say chile you are not pure after having a baby," Dream joked and I stuck my middle finger up at her causing us to laugh.

"Ladiesssssssss," we heard a voice sing out and we turned in the direction of the door to see Joi standing there looking as good as ever.

"JOI!" we all called out in unison as we embraced her with a group hug.

"I've missed you, girls."

"How have you been?" Satin asked her with a smile on her face.

"I've been okay. Moving was the best thing that happened to me."

"You like South Carolina?"

"South Carolina has been great to me honestly. It's definitely an experience. After everything that happened, I needed to go away and escape everything that reminded me of home. I'm sorry for skipping out on you all without a goodbye. I still regret that."

"You don't have to apologize. We understood. You did what you felt was best for you and we can never get upset with you over that," I said as I dried the tear that had fallen from her eyes.

"I love you ladies so much, you have no idea."

****

I am ready for love. All of the joy and the pain, and all the time

that it takes just to stay in your good grace. Lately, I've been thinking

maybe you're not ready for me. Maybe you think I need to learn

maturity. They say watch what you ask for cause you might receive.

But if you ask me tomorrow, I'll say the same thing. I am ready for

love. Would you please lend me your ear? I promise I won't complain.

I just need you to acknowledge I am here.

As I made my way down the aisle to Sincere I couldn't help but cry tears of joy. I was getting ready to marry the man of my life and it felt so surreal. I've waited for this moment my entire life and here it was. I planned my wedding in my head as a little girl and now as a woman, I was making my dream a reality.

I had everything I could have possibly asked for. A great family. Amazing friends. A wonderful man who I was getting ready to marry. Life was beautiful.

Shifting my attention to the beautiful little girl who rested comfortably in Dreams arms I smiled at my greatest accomplishment yet. I was a mother to the prettiest little human being I've laid eyes on. After the discovery of finding out that Sincere was indeed hiding my birth control, we found out that I was already 18 weeks pregnant. Turns out I conceived the night he proposed. Imagine my surprise when the doctor told me that. I wasn't ready to be a mother but now that I am I don't remember what life was like before her.

Finally making my way to the alter I stopped before turning to look at Sincere and said a silent prayer to God. I had to thank him for sending him to me. For blessing me with an amazing man to love me despite my flaws. No matter what we went through this man has never left my side. As he grabbed ahold of both of my hands we smiled at one another while the pastor spoke his speech.

By the time we said I do, I was a crying mess. I didn't care about my makeup being ruined all I cared about was starting my forever with my best friend. With the love of my life. He was created for me. He was who God had chosen for me and he honestly couldn't have chosen a better person. Sincere was everything to me and I had no plans of ever letting him go. Maybe fairytales do exist after all.

Joi

Isabella and Sincere wedding was beautiful. It made me revisit my own wedding day and I should've known my marriage was gonna be doomed. Our wedding day was horrible. Jacob had gotten pissy drunk the night before and when it was time for me to walk down the aisle he was nowhere to be found and I was so embarrassed. Anyways that was a clear indication that we were making a mistake yet I ignored it.

I still believed love was beautiful regardless of how things had played out. Jacob just wasn't the man for me no matter how much I tried to make him be. We weren't right for each other yet I forced it and in return, I was left with heartache that could've been avoided. I could've saved myself from everything I endured in those twelve years.

Unfortunately the baby I was carrying was born stillborn. I had a hard time accepting that I was carrying his child and once I became okay with it I went into a premature labor. I never heard my child cry. I never saw him smile. And I'll never forget that.

After all of that happened I packed up and went to South Carolina. I needed a change of scenery. I needed to be around a group of different people. People I didn't know. I just needed and wanted a fresh start.

"Thank you for coming," Isabella said as she walked up to me in a different dress.

"You don't have to thank me. You knew I was coming. Nothing would keep me from witnessing this," I said to her sincerely.

"I know but I know what painful memories reside here, you know? There's a reason why you left. I just hate that we couldn't do more for you."

"Izzy there's nothing nobody could have done. I had to get right with myself. I had to come to terms with the way things had turned out to be on my own."

"I admire you so much. You have no idea girly."

"Stop! You're always bringing out the emotional side of me," I told her as I laughed.

"I've always been the emotional one. I can't help it. I'm just so freaking happy to see you. I haven't saw that smile in so long. I missed it," she said just as Sincere walked over to us handing her the baby.

"Hey Aubrey, met aunty Joi," she said and Aubrey just buried her head into her chest.

"She's so adorable. I can't believe you're a mother. You should've saw my face when I was scrolling down IG and came across this little beauty and saw that you had posted her."

"Yeah, I still can't believe I'm a mother either. I find myself just smiling at her as I watch her sleep like a creep. I never knew that I could love someone the way I love her. She gave me a purpose."

"I can only imagine," I told her as I caught myself getting emotional.

"Hey, it'll happen when it's supposed to. Some man will come along someday and whisk you away and you won't even remember what life was like without him because he'll complete you. I love you, okay?" she spoke to me and I simply gave her a small smile letting her know I understood before she walked away, I'm assuming to find her husband.

I never in my life imagined that my life would be what it has turned out to be. I lost my husband. I lost my best friend but I still kept pushing. I went through a lot of heartache and pain but I'm still standing. I'm still living and able to see another day. Every day I wake up I'm blessed to have a second chance to rewrite my story.

So what Isabella just said to me was right. One day I will know what it's like to find my life partner and when that happens I welcome it. I welcome all things positive. Until then I'll cherish life as I know it now. I'll cherish and embrace it for as long as I live. So my story may not have the perfect happy ending and that's okay. My story is still being written.

Dream

"Why do you keep lookin' at me like that?" Mega asked me as we sat next to each other watching everyone cut up on the dance floor.

"Looking at you like what?" I asked back smiling.

"I don't know. You just keep lookin' at me with that silly grin plastered on your face."

"I can't look at you? I can't look at you and admire how fine you are in your suit?"

"You tryna get fucked talkin' like that. You know it ain't nothing for me to take you somewhere and lift up that dress. You know ya man makes shit happen."

"Why must you be so nasty?"

"You got me this way."

"Lies. You got yourself that way. Every time I walk in the house you try getting some booty and I never thought I'd say this but I'm sexed out. I need a new coochie," I joked.

"Nah Dreamy that be you. You almost broke my dick the other night. A nigga almost thought he was out of commission for a second," he said back to me causing me to laugh.

"I did not. All I wanted to do was get some loving but you couldn't keep up."

"Dream I gave yo ass two rounds. Fuck you want from me? You want to fuck all the time you better go get you a young nigga."

"I just may have to. Your geriatric ass got bad knees and hips. You all messed up."

"Yo did you just call me geriatric?" he asked cracking up.

"Yupp. You my little geriatric gangsta."

Mega and I were still going strong. In fact, I took him up on his offer and moved down to Florida with him. We didn't move to Miami though, I didn't want to stay there so we found us a nice five bedroom house out in Fort Lauderdale and I loved it. It just seemed like the perfect place for us.

He and Hassan ended up partnering with the strip club and it was doing very well. I, unfortunately, wasn't working but I helped them out a lot at the club so I wasn't just out there doing nothing. I will admit that I missed my girls though especially Satin. So when Isabella sent her wedding invite I knew it was a must to attend.

It felt good to be back home. I missed Springfield. I was born and raised here and despite all the crazy shit I went through growing up I would go through it again if it led me to this moment right here. It was all worth it because I found my soulmate in Mega.

He's not perfect and I later found out he had a whole baby on the side and I ain't even gonna lie I went the fuck off. I'm talking vandalizing cars, breaking shit in our house, hell I even cut him. I was livid, but we managed to work through it and get past it.

We'll never find the perfect partner but we will find the perfect partner to go through hell and high water with. The day I met him my life changed for the better. I was going through life hurt and alone since I didn't have my parents and I was the only child but Satin came along and filled a void of emptiness I had and once I met Mega he completed me. My heart was whole again.

"You aight?" he asked me breaking me out of my thoughts.

"I'm fine bae."

"You sure? You spaced out for a second. You sure everything is good?"

"I'm positive. Everything for once in my life is perfect. Everything is just perfect," I told him as I leaned in to give him a kiss making sure to kiss him with everything in me. I was trying to transfer all of my love and emotion into him so that he could feel me. Feel all of me without being inside of me.

Breaking our kiss I just gazed into his eyes and silently thanked God for sending him to me. For trusting me with this man's heart. I was his for as long as he wanted to have me and from the looks of it that would be forever.

I was happy. Like genuinely happy and I was finally living my best life.

Satin

Where do I begin? I managed to finish cosmetology school despite all the craziness. After my grandmother died I made it my business to make her proud. It wasn't easy but I managed to get it done. I was so uninspired to go on and even contemplated suicide but every time I went to swallow the little pill cocktail I had made up I always heard her voice and I snapped out of it. I wasn't raised to be some weak shell of a woman yet I was acting like one.

I lost sight of everything and gave up on life but Renee was there every step of the way. Maybe it was out of guilt. Maybe it was out of love but either way, she was there and I appreciated her for that. We were still trying to work on our relationship though. As much as she has been there for me I was still kind of hesitant to let her in my world completely. I just kept wondering what if she just up and disappeared on me again. I couldn't handle that so I figured if I kept her at bay I wouldn't get hurt.

Her revelation about Kori still shocked the hell out of me every day. My whole life I thought he, well she was my cousin and come to find out we were brother and sister. I missed Kori. I missed her a lot. Her murder went on to be unsolved and I had to come to terms that I may never get that closure on who did it and why. In the back of my mind, I suspected Jacob but I guess we'll never know seeing how a dead man can't talk.

Making my way across the room I spotted this little cutie who seemed to grab my attention since I saw him at the ceremony earlier. I was gonna shoot my shot with his little fine ass. Once I made it to where he was at I smiled before saying hello.

"Wassup?" he asked me flashing a beautiful smile with the prettiest white teeth I have ever seen.

"You," I flirted back.

"You here with anybody?"

"Actually I am. And no disrespect I don't really want no trouble with my ol' lady lil mama."

"What you scared of?"

"I'm not scared of anything but you should be."

"Is that right?" I told him stepping closer into his personal space barely leaving room between the two of us.

"Guess it's a good thing you came with me then, huh?"

"I guess you're right," Hassan said back as he wrapped his arms around my waist.

"How did we end up here?"

"You. You stole my heart and ran off with it. Had me changing everything I swore by."

"You knew you had to get your shit together or I wasn't fucking with you. I meant that shit."

"Why you so mean?" he asked laughing.

"I'm not mean. I'm just not one for the bullshit. Like how did you think my black ass was going for that poly bullshit? You know black girls ain't with all that. Talking about 'it's my lifestyle'. You pissed me off that day," I responded as I giggled.

"I got you now though so I ain't really trippin'."

"I bet!"

"I can't wait until I'm waking up next to you every day."

"Soon my love. Soon!"

"Big booty come on so we can take this group photo," Dream said to me as she and the other girls came over interrupting Hassan and I moment.

"Y'all heffas see me over here boo loving and y'all want to mess everything up," I complained just before placing a kiss on his lips.

"Bitch suck his dick later. Let's take this damn picture," Dream fussed and we all laughed.

"I don't suck dick but I hear you're the real headmaster."

"Headmaster huh? Shit got a nice ring to it don't it Dreamy," Mega said and Dream rolled her eyes.

"Mega please don't entertain her shenanigans if you want some neck anytime soon. I'm warning you," Dream said to him and he put his hands up in a surrender gesture.

"Some things don't change I see," Joi commented.

"Not with these two," Isabella said with a giggle.

This reminded me of all the good times we shared. We probably didn't all talk every day but we kept in touch and our sisterhood was still very much intact. These women weren't just my friends they were my sisters and I couldn't imagine life without them.

As far as Hassan and I go, we were finally working on our relationship. Once he saw that I wasn't with that poly bullshit he got rid of everyone for little ol' me and I knew that I had made a great choice in giving this thing a try. And since I had sold my childhood home I had decided to take a leap of faith and move down to Miami to be with him. I was popping up on Dream's doorstep like 'I'm here bihhhhhh'. Shhh, don't tell her that though.

I was going to Florida and beginning a new life. I was going to open up that Salon Kori and I was supposed to open together and begin living. Most people don't live, they exist. I no longer wanted to exist, I wanted to live and I planned on doing just that.

I'm not sure what the future holds for me or for my friends but I think I speak for everyone when I say life was pretty amazing for us all. We've experienced ups and downs but we still prevailed no matter the situation. You see what happens when you get a bunch of bad bitches together and they link up? They support one another and stick together. Our bond was unbreakable and I wouldn't have it any other way.

The End

CPSIA information can be obtained
at www.ICGtesting.com
Printed in the USA
LVHW112020121218
600231LV00001B/53/P